D1489026

At Low Tide

Carrie Watson

Copyright © 2012 Carrie Watson

All rights reserved.

ISBN-10: 1479255025
ISBN-13: 978-1479255023

DEDICATION

To my family, I am lucky to have you all in my life. You give me love, support, and the encouragement to follow my dreams. To my Dad, you taught me that anything is possible. To Ross, you are my heart and my best friend. This book is especially dedicated to my Mom who not only gave me so many of the wonderful things I have in this world, but who is also there for me no matter what. I love you.

ACKNOWLEDGMENTS

This book would not have been possible if it weren't for the technical editing of Ross Bacon and the revision critiques of Barbara McGuigan.

It was because of my creative editor Danielle Watson that I decided to pursue writing this book. She is my sister and my biggest fan.

i

Chapter 1

Ryan sat in the waiting room of the doctor's office flipping through a fishing magazine. He wasn't really reading it or even looking at the pictures, just turning page by page to give his hands something to do. There were only two other people there. An elderly woman sat across the room next to a man who Ryan assumed was her husband. She was wearing a scarf around her head since it looked like she had lost most of her hair.

The door next to the reception window opened and a nurse stood in the doorway. The nurse looked directly at Ryan.

"Mr. Westin?"

"Yes."

"You can come back now."

Ryan put the magazine back on the rack where he had gotten it from and followed the nurse through the door. She turned left and he walked behind her down the long hallway. She stopped at the last door on the right. She opened the door, but didn't walk in. She smiled politely and gestured for Ryan to go in. When he walked into the small exam room, she shut the door behind him.

"Doctor Franklin, this is my son Ryan."

Ryan looked from his father sitting on the exam table to the man in the white coat sitting at the small wooden desk. He had never seen his father as anything but a strong man, one that people would only dare to reckon with, even though he was as gentle as they come on the inside. Like Ryan, he had worked in the construction business all of his life.

Seeing him sitting there on the exam table though, he looked small somehow. It was as if his father hadn't aged a day since Ryan was five years old, but in the twenty minutes that Ryan was in the waiting room, his father aged the twenty years that Ryan hadn't noticed until that day. His hair looked a lighter shade of grey and his wrinkles were more distinguishable.

Dr. Franklin stood up and extended his hand. "Ryan, it's nice to meet you. I'm Dr. Franklin."

Ryan shook his hand. "It's nice to meet you as well."

"Please, have a seat."

"Thank you."

"Your father and I were just going over his test results. The tests we ran showed that your father has pancreatic cancer."

Ryan looked at the doctor and tried to process his words. He took a long, slow breath before he asked him "Is it treatable?"

"There are four stages of pancreatic cancer with one being the earliest, least advanced stage. Your father is in stage three, so unfortunately surgery is no longer an option."

Ryan's father interrupted the doctor. "Son, I'm dying. There are no ifs, ands, or butts about it."

Ryan closed his eyes and pinched the bridge of his nose. He did this whenever he was confused or frustrated. He opened his eyes and looked from his father back to Dr. Franklin. "How long?"

"Well, if your father went through rounds of chemotherapy and radiation it would treat the symptoms and give him some more time. He could live for another three or four years."

Ryan's father didn't give the doctor a chance to continue. "Yeah and be sick as a dog for those years. No thanks, Doc. I watched my best friend Don go through all that with doctors pumping him full of one chemical after another. That's not for me."

"Dad, can we at least listen to what the doctor has to say?"

"Dr. Franklin said that without treatment, I'll have another two years."

Ryan looked at Dr. Franklin, who responded, "At best. It's more likely to be closer to one."

His father ignored the doctor and continued. "I am sixty-four years old. I am going to spend whatever time I got left on this Earth fishing and helping you learn how to run Westin Construction. Then, I'm going to go and see your mother. God rest her soul."

About thirty minutes later, Ryan and his father walked out of the doctor's office and got into Ryan's truck.

"Dad, can we at least discuss this?"

"We already did. There's nothing left to discuss. Plus, I have to get back to the office. Next week I want you to appoint a new foreman to take over your crew. There are a lot of things that you need to learn before you become the president of the company."

"Why don't I move back home with you? With all of the work I've done to my house, I can probably sell it for almost twice what I paid for it."

"What for? I don't need you coming home and taking up all my free space. Plus, you put so much work into that house that it would be a shame to let some stranger buy it. What if they come in and paint the walls purple or something?" His father smiled at him from the passenger seat.

"You might need some help eventually. It would be better if I just came back and lived with you."

"No, you stay right where you're at. I'll be just fine. Plus, you don't want to come live with a dying old man. What you *should* do is find a pretty young girl to live with you in that house. You're almost as good looking as I was at your age, so you shouldn't be having so much trouble finding a young lady who's as nice as she is easy on the eyes to spend your time with."

Ryan just smiled and rolled his eyes at his dad's lack of modesty as he turned onto the highway. His father insisted that Ryan drop him off at his house in New Jersey so he could get his own truck before he went back to work in Northeast Philadelphia.

About a month later, Ryan was lying in his bed watching TV. He was exhausted after a long day. Somehow the nine hour days he was spending in the office with his father were more exhausting than the ten hour days he used to spend out on the job site. He liked working on site so much better. He had been a good foreman and all of his guys both liked and respected him. He had thought that it would be ten more years before his dad would retire and he would take over for him.

Ryan was just starting to doze off at eleven o'clock when his cell phone rang and made him jolt awake. Ryan picked up the phone.

"Hello... Yes, speaking... An accident? ...What happened? Ok, I'll be right there... Thank you."

Ryan put on a clean shirt, grabbed his wallet, cell phone, and keys, and hurried out to his truck. As he drove over the bridge he couldn't help thinking that he should have went to live with his father. A month after his father was diagnosed with terminal cancer he had a car accident. *If I had been there, I could have gone out for him. Where was he even going? He was probably only going out to pick up ice cream or something. That man has a sweet tooth larger than anyone I know.*

His father was a wonderful man, but he could also be so stubborn. Ryan knew that if he had tried to move in with him that his father would have probably just waited until Ryan left for work one day and then had someone come to change the locks. People did things his way whether they wanted to or not. Ryan wondered if he would ever be able to do as good of a job running his father's construction company as he did. But first, Ryan had to focus on getting to the hospital to make sure his dad was alright.

Ryan arrived at the hospital twenty minutes later. A nurse led him through the winding hallways to an office where there was a policeman standing outside the door. Ryan knew it wasn't a good sign that they were bringing him there and not to see his father. The policeman led Ryan into the office where there was a doctor sitting at his desk.

"Hello, Mr. Westin. I'm Officer Angeloni."

"I'm Doctor Walters. Please have a seat."

Ryan sat down in the chair across the desk from the doctor and the officer took the seat by the wall and turned his chair to face Ryan's.

Officer Angeloni spoke first. "As you know, your father was in a car accident. He was pulling out of a 7-11 parking lot and was hit by a drunk driver who ran a red light. The witnesses who saw the accident said that when your father's car was rear-ended that it went forward into a street light. We were able to get him out of the car and into an ambulance. He was still conscious at that point, but he lost consciousness in the ambulance on the way here."

Ryan's eyes filled with moisture, but he closed them and took a deep breath. "Is he dead?"

Dr. Walters responded, "Yes, I'm sorry Mr. Westin. They tried to revive him in the ambulance, but when they wheeled him into the emergency room, there was nothing we could do. He was already gone. I'm sorry."

"Thank you Doctor, me too." It was all Ryan could think of to say. Ryan sat there for a moment and then turned to Officer Angeloni. "What about the driver in the other car?"

"He survived. One of my fellow officers is with him. Once he is released from the hospital, the driver of the car will be taken to the station as he is already under arrest."

A nurse came in and took Ryan to see his father and then gave him all of the paperwork that needed to be filled out. When Ryan got home at four thirty in the morning, he had too much to do before trying to get any sleep.

Chapter 2

Three years later…

After his father passed, Ryan took over running the company much sooner than he was ready to. His father had only spent a little over a week going through all the responsibilities that would be falling on him, so for the past three years Ryan did the best that he could while learning on the job. Unfortunately, Ryan wasn't born with the natural business sense his father had and had landed himself in trouble. Enough trouble in fact, that Ryan had spent a few long nights in jail. A few days after he was released, a man he didn't know came to see him. He gave Ryan a card with an address on it and told him he was requested to be there at the time written.

At ten o'clock on a Friday morning in late June, Ryan walked up the long, winding brick pathway to the front door of a huge, colonial style house. He reached up, rang the doorbell, and then stepped back to wait. The door opened and a large man stood there filling the doorway. He had an enormous stature and his very presence was intimidating, but Ryan knew that before he even knocked on the door.

"Ah, Ryan Westin. Come in. My office is back here. Can I get you something to drink?"

"No, thank you. I'm fine."

Ryan followed the man through the foyer and down the long hallway. The man opened the last door on the left and asked him to please come in and take a seat. Ryan did as requested, but remained quiet. The man walked to the other side of the desk and sat down. Behind him was a large bay window. The light coming in from behind him slightly shadowed his face. The man sitting across the desk from him was Harold Shaw. He was the District Attorney of Investigations of Northeast Philadelphia.

"Westin, do you know why I asked you here?"

"No Sir, I don't. I know you instructed me not to bring my attorney, but I really don't feel comfortable being here without him. It doesn't seem appropriate."

"You are a smarter man than I gave you credit for. You're right, it would be completely inappropriate. That's why we're just having a pleasant conversation from one businessman to another. There are no records being taken here, no cameras, or recorders. And if you by any chance have one on your person I will find out about it."

"I don't have anything on me. Is there a reason why I should have tried to bring one?"

"Not at all."

"Then why would you bring it up?"

"I'm a very careful man."

They both sat there and eyed each other carefully. Ryan didn't know what to say next. He wasn't sure if he should ask the obvious question yet or let Shaw keep talking.

When Shaw sat there in silence, Ryan decided to ask, "Why is it that you asked me here, Mr. Shaw?"

"What if I told you that I was the one who made sure that your bail was posted, so that you would be released from jail?"

"Why would you do that when you were the one who made the decision to approve the charges made against me? Why would you pay that kind of money to bail me out?"

"How were those few nights in jail, Westin?"

"To put it nicely… they were unpleasant, but you didn't answer my question."

"So I'm assuming you don't want to go back there ever again."

"Who in their right mind would want that?" Ryan started to become frustrated that Shaw wasn't giving him the information he wanted.

"Well, that's exactly where you're going."

Ryan tried to keep his voice calm and level. "I didn't do anything wrong."

"Oh, yes you did. But I can make it go away and make sure you never spend another minute in jail for the rest of your life. I just need you to do me a little favor."

"What kind of favor?"

Shaw turned his chair around and reached for a blank manila folder on his credenza behind him. He turned back to Ryan and handed it to him across the desk. Ryan took it and sat back in his chair. He didn't open it. He just sat back and waited. He knew that he should just get up and leave. Once he opened the folder, he couldn't un-open it.

"Is there a problem?"

"No, there's no problem."

"I didn't think so, considering the answers to all of your problems are right there in that file. What I'm asking you to do is very simple."

Ryan opened the folder and studied its contents carefully. Shaw sat across the desk and studied Ryan as he looked through the items and read Shaw's proposal.

"I can't…"

"…give me an answer right now? Of course you can't! And I wouldn't expect you to. A wise businessman can't make a decision in two minutes, even if it *is* an overly generous offer."

"My father told me to look out for things that are too good to be true."

"I knew your father. He was a smart man. If you were as smart as he was, then you wouldn't be sitting here in my office. He never made the mistakes you've made. But everyone is allowed to make mistakes, as long as they pay for them. You can pay for yours by helping me out with this little matter or you can pay your debt to society. That's up to you. I want you to give me an answer by next week."

Ryan closed the folder and handed it back to Shaw. "I will give you an answer by Wednesday."

"Good enough. When you decide, you can reach me at this number." Shaw opened the desk drawer next to him. He pulled out a business card and handed it to Ryan. "Remember, you don't have to do this. I am a big believer in letting justice prevail, especially when I'm on my side determining what's just." Shaw laughed.

"I'll see myself out. Have a good day, Mr. Shaw."

"You too, Westin."

Ryan left the house and walked back to his truck. The driveway was large enough to turn his truck around and drive forward out of it. He turned onto the road and drove about a block before he pulled over. He took out his cell phone, scrolled through the contacts list, selected a number, and pressed send.

"Hey Matt, it's Ryan... I'm doing ok... Listen, I was wondering if anyone was renting your beach house this week... I need to go somewhere to relax and clear my head... Thanks... Yeah it's a mess right now, but it will all get cleared up... No, of course I wouldn't mind. It's the least I can do. I'll bring my tools with me... Great, I'll be by to pick up the keys. Listen Man, I really appreciate this." Ryan hung up the phone. He put his truck back into drive and started to head toward Matt's house.

Ryan arrived at the beach house late in the afternoon. It had been a long ride. As Ryan moved slowly down the highway with the weekend traffic he replayed the meeting with Shaw over and over in his mind. He thought about whether or not he could actually do what Shaw had asked. Driving to the shore was the first step, but he wasn't sure he could take anymore. He also thought about ways in which he could either complete the task or get around it somehow and still not go to jail.

Ryan had forgotten to eat that day, so after he put his bag in the bedroom at the house, he went back out to get some food and a case of beer. After a beer and a sandwich, he decided to go for a walk down to the beach.

Chapter 3

Nicolette drew in a deep breath of salty air as she walked along the trail through the reed covered dunes. Pebbles were scattered under her feet, so she waited until she got to the edge of the sand to take off her flip-flops. The dunes drifted behind her and her view cleared. All she could see was sand and ocean.

Once she reached the edge of the water, she walked to the north end of the beach where the island came to a point. Her toes were only a few feet from the ocean, but she could also turn around and watch the bay slowly sucking the red sun down into it to beyond the west side of the island behind the lighthouse in the distance. It was her favorite place, where she came in the summer time to find peace and quiet.

She carried her flip-flops, one in each hand. Her mesh shorts and t-shirt blew in the breeze that swept the ocean onto the beach. Only this place could dull the ringing in her ears. It hushed her mother from clanging the dinner dishes in the sink and her sisters and sisters-in-law chatting and laughing around the dining room table over coffee. It quieted the sound of all the children's high-pitched screams as they ran away from her brother, "The Uncle Frank Monster." Her father's snores coming from the living room couch were silenced more with each crashing wave.

Nicolette loved her family. Every year she looked forward to meeting them in the summer at their parent's beach house. But by the end of the first week, she started to find excuses to sneak away for an hour or two at a time after dinner. This year, she had made it all the way to Friday.

Her oldest brother Jerry and his wife Natalie had two kids, Maya and Nathan, who were five and three years old. After Jerry, her parents had Stephanie. Stephanie and her husband Pete had a four year old named Noah and a three year old named Jordan. Next was her brother Frank. He was married to Lisa. They didn't have any kids, *God bless them*. Although that could have also been why Frank thought nothing of getting his nieces and nephews all riled up just before bed time.

Then of course there were her sisters, the twins. The twins had always excelled at everything. They were all-state softball and basketball players in high school, and they were all-conference in basketball at St. Joe's University in Philadelphia. One twin, Marie, had just gotten married during the previous summer to her college sweetheart Joe. Marie told Nicolette they had been trying to get pregnant since a month after their honeymoon. Ironically Caitlyn, the twin who wasn't married, just found out that she was pregnant. Her brothers and sisters all knew, but none of them wanted to be there when she told their mother.

"It's still better than being twenty-nine and single." Caitlyn had blurted out earlier that day while Nicolette and her brothers and sisters were all sitting on the beach. She liked to take cheap shots at Nicolette whenever she got the chance.

Without even sitting up in her chair or moving at all, Nicolette replied "Which is much better than being thirty-one, unmarried, and knocked up."

"At least I have a boyfriend. And a boyfriend who didn't…"

"Caitlyn!" Nicolette's brother Frank cut her off. "Don't be such a bitch."

"Yeah that's too far, Cate." Marie chimed in. "Let's talk about something else."

"Talk about whatever you want. I'm going for a swim." Cate stood from her spot in the middle of the semi-circle of chairs and walked down to the water.

"And the hormones begin to rear their ugly

heads." Jerry laughed.

"At least she'll have that as an excuse for the next seven months. It doesn't explain the last few decades though." Frank said.

"And forget about what she said, Nicky. You'll find someone soon enough, but you should really try getting yourself out there more." Stephanie added.

Nicolette was the youngest. She didn't have any kids and she wasn't married. She hadn't even had any prospects in a long time. Her sisters didn't let her forget it either. Maybe that was why she took walks to the beach after dinner.

She had only been with one man in the past three years. He had taken her out on a date about a year ago and they had a nice time. A few glasses of wine accompanied dinner, so she agreed to go to his house for coffee after they left the restaurant. She knew that even though he was a nice guy that he wasn't just asking her there to have coffee. She was sure that he had gotten the impression that they had clicked instantly. But actually she had just been overly agreeable and friendly. She wasn't really a fan of hockey and basketball and horror movies, it just made the evening easier and more fun if she just agreed and said she liked all the same stuff he did. She was trying to move on and that was more important.

When she got to his apartment, he made his move and she went through the motions. She thought maybe if she forced herself through the beginning that maybe it would get easier after that.

She hadn't made love with a man for two years. With her mind and body not fully engaged, it seemed awkward and bumpy. The foreplay felt more like a chore. She tried making love to him, but she was thankful that the lights were off so that he wouldn't notice the bored look on her face, since she was only pretending. She just wanted to try to get back out there.

Nicolette sat on the beach and thought about that night a little over a year ago. The sun was almost completely gone. She thought about getting up and walking back to the house, but decided to stay a few more minutes. She was thinking about how much she enjoyed the way the breeze brushed her face when her thoughts were interrupted by footsteps splashing through the foam of the waves at the edge of the water behind her.

Chapter 4

Nicolette turned and saw a man walking, looking out over the ocean. Whether it was starting to get too dark, or he was too distracted, he didn't see her sitting in the sand about ten or fifteen yards away. She cleared her throat so that he would look up and realize that she was there. It made him jump. Nicolette hadn't meant to scare him. *At least I know that for a stranger he's not dangerous, since he jumps at the slightest noise.*

As he walked by he looked up at her for a brief second. Then he looked a second time in a surprised kind of way and crossed the two second timeframe that went from looking to starring, at least in

Nicolette's opinion.

"Hello." He said before he quickly put his head down again.

"Hi." Nicolette replied and was happy to leave it at a simple, polite greeting. She still felt like being alone. Or at least she would have, but when he side glanced at her to acknowledge her greeting he didn't see the water swell up behind him. She opened her mouth and tried to warn him, but before any sound came out a wave pulled his feet out from under him and he toppled over in the shallow water as another wave washed over him and onto the beach.

Nicolette jumped up and ran over. She grabbed him by the arm to help him up. As much as she tried to hold it in, she couldn't help laughing a little. She tried not to let him see though.

"Are you ok?"

He coughed a few times before he said, "I'd be a little better if I didn't feel like I just swallowed half of the ocean... And if you hadn't seen me fall." He stood all the way up and wiped his face. "*AND* if you weren't laughing at me."

Nicolette couldn't hold it back any longer. She let the laughter out. In between chuckles she managed to apologize. "I'm sorry, but if you could have seen yourself. I shouldn't laugh though. Please don't be embarrassed. It could have happened to anyone."

The man started laughing as well. "Maybe not

anyone. You won't find many people who are less graceful than I am, so I should at least get *some* credit for that."

"Ok, that's fair."

They both stopped laughing and he introduced himself. "I'm Ryan." He said as he extended his hand.

"Nicolette. It's nice to meet you." She shook his hand and then walked over to the spot she had been sitting in.

"Can I join you?"

"Umm… Sure, I guess. Although, I don't know. Is it safe to sit near you?"

"Probably not, but that's just a chance you'll have to take."

"I owe you one anyway. I needed a good laugh tonight."

"Glad I could help." Ryan plopped down in the sand about a foot away from Nicolette. It was still a little closer than she would have liked.

They sat there for a minute. Ryan was still trying to catch his breath. Once he did, he was the first to speak again.

"So how come you were sitting out here by yourself?"

"I like the beach at night. It's quiet and

peaceful. Why were you out here?"

"Same reason I guess. I used to come here all the time and I missed it, so I thought I would come and take a walk and put my feet in the water."

"Well you succeeded in doing that."

"Yeah I guess I did." Ryan laughed. "Are you here on vacation?"

"You could say that. My parents live here at the shore and my brothers, sisters and I all come and visit for a little over a month every summer. It gets kind of crazy in the house though, so I come out here to get a break from all the chaos."

"How many brothers and sisters do you have?"

"Two brothers, three sisters, two sisters-in-law, two brothers-in-law, one niece, three nephews, and another on the way."

"Wow. Is that all?" Ryan turned and looked at her with his eyes wide.

"Plus myself and my parents. If it didn't get so cold on the beach at night, I would be tempted to set up a tent and sleep here."

"It must be nice having such a big family though." He said turning to look back at the ocean.

"You're family must be different from mine."

"I never had much family, only my dad really."

"Oh. Not even cousins or anything?"

25

"My parents didn't have brothers or sisters. Each of them was an only child. I was an only child too. My mom died when I was young and my dad died a few years ago."

Guilt plucked Nicolette's chest. "I'm sorry. If I would have known, I wouldn't have complained."

"Don't worry about it. What street do your parents live on?"

Nicolette didn't answer. She just turned and looked at him with a questionable expression.

"What?"

"I'm not going to tell you that. I just met you five seconds ago. I have no idea who you are."

"I wasn't going to start stalking you or anything. I was just making conversation."

"I know, but for all I know you could be a crazy serial killer or something. Although, you probably wouldn't be a good one, since you might have trouble holding a knife and walking at the same time, but you never know."

"It's obvious that you're the trusting type." His said sarcastically. "Even if I was a serial killer though, I wouldn't kill you."

"Oh yeah? Why is that?"

"Because you saved my life."

"I saved your life? How do you figure that?"

"I could have drowned. It's a good thing you were here."

Nicolette smiled for the first time since she had stopped laughing. "You weren't going to drown. After the wave knocked you over you were in a foot of water."

"A person can drown in only one inch of water though. It's possible."

"Well then it was a good thing I was here."

"I'm glad you were." Ryan smiled at Nicolette.

Nicolette tensed up and didn't know how to respond to that. He was a very good looking man. He wasn't overly tall, but still about six or seven inches taller than she was. He was slender, well dressed, and clean cut with a smooth face. Even in the dark, she could tell he was nicely tanned. Despite his good looks, instead of feeling an attraction, she started to get that panicked feeling again. The most she could manage to sputter out was, "Oh… thanks, but… I, um…"

"I'm sorry. I just meant you're nice to talk to. Plus, you probably have a boyfriend or something right?"

"No. I did, but it's not something I really like talking about."

"Ok, it's no problem. We can talk about something else. Hmmm… The weather is a safe topic. You were right about it getting cold here at night."

Nicolette turned and looked at Ryan. He was shivering from sitting in the wind while he was soaking wet. "Oh my God, you're freezing. Are you far from where you're staying? My parents' house isn't too far. I can run and get you a towel or something if you want."

"I'm ok. I don't want to have to keep my eyes closed the whole time because you wouldn't want me to see where you lived."

"You're not going to let that go are you?"

"Nope. I should be going anyway. Nicolette, it was very nice meeting you." Ryan said as he stood up.

"Same here."

"Hopefully we'll run into each other again."

"Have a good night."

Nicolette sat and stared out over the water for a minute and then turned to look to see which direction Ryan had walked in, but she couldn't see him anywhere down the beach. Either he had turned up one of the street walkways through the dunes or it was just too dark to see very far. Wherever he went, he disappeared really quickly.

It was the first time in a while that she had met someone new and enjoyed his company as much as she had. *I probably could have toned down being my cold, distant self. I hate that I do that. He was perfectly nice.* She let the thoughts leave her mind as quickly as they had entered and then she started to feel almost lighthearted - *probably because I had such a good laugh.* She smiled to herself a little, got up, and started to walk down the beach toward 3rd Street where her parents' house was.

"Nicky? Niiiiiiiiick?"

"Over here, Frank!"

Frank had just walked onto the beach from the 3rd Street entrance when Nicolette heard him calling for her. She waved to him, but he didn't wave back, just nodded his head at her. She knew he must have been worried.

"What's up, Kid? What are you doing out here so late? Are you crazy?"

"You don't have to worry about me, Frank. I'm a big girl."

"Oh ok, well then I'll put it in my calendar to remind myself to stop next week," he said as he put his arm around her shoulders. "You don't have to come out here and hide all night. I know the twins can be bitches, Cate especially, but the rest of us aren't so bad are we?"

"You know it's not that."

"Yeah I know. Plus, I had to get out of there for a little bit too. The kids are really hyper and Stephanie and Natalie can't get them to settle down and go to sleep, so everyone is pretty ticked off at me right now. Why don't we walk over to 4th Street and get some ice cream at Dairy Delight before we walk back?"

"Sure. We should bring some back for the kids too. Then they'll never sleep." Nicolette laughed.

"You're so evil. I love it." He kissed her on the top of her head. "But I don't feel like paying for ice cream Stephanie and Natalie will just end up making me wear."

That night Nicolette tried to fall asleep on the pull out couch in the attic. There were no bedrooms left in the house, and even Caitlyn had to share a room with bunk beds and an air mattress with Marie and her husband. As Nicolette lied there she thought of how she met Ryan on the beach. They got along great and she felt very comfortable around him until he started to show the slightest bit of interest in her. Then her stomach tightened, she felt short of breath and she put up her icy wall. She wondered if she would ever be able to get over those feelings. She had even tried going to counseling for about six months, but that didn't help. Her counselor was really odd and also completely useless.

Just as Nicolette drifted off to sleep, she heard loud screeching tires, a loud thunderous crash, and glass shattering and scattering across asphalt. In a flash she was in a hospital. EMTs rushed by her pushing people on stretchers covered in blood-stained white sheets. She tried to run after them, but her feet wouldn't move quickly enough. They ran through a wooden door that shut in her face. A female judge walked by her dressed in her black robes. She pushed past Nicolette and banged on the door three times with her gavel.

The loud banging made Nicolette stir in her bed

and she could no longer see the hospital, the door, or the judge. She could only see emptiness behind her eyelids. Suddenly, she heard the rhythmic banging again and she shot straight up in her bed. She tried to wipe the sweat from her face.

"Knock, knock, knock! Aunt Nicky! Mommom wants everyone to come down to breakfast! Wake up, Aunt Nicky!"

"Ok Maya, I'll be right there Sweetie."

At one point she had gotten used to the nightmares. They used to happen all the time until they finally had become sporadic. *Come to think of it, I haven't had one in months.*

Nicolette rubbed her eyes and got up. She got dressed and pulled her hair back. Then, she walked over to the trap door in the floor, pushed down on it, and unfolded the ladder so she could carefully descend to the third floor. Leaning against the wall was the broom that Maya had affectively used as an alarm clock. Nicolette folded the stairs back up and could see the scuff marks from the broom when she pushed the trap door shut in the ceiling.

Chapter 5

Ryan's eyes squinted as the sun rose into the window next to his bed. He rolled over and buried his face into the pillow. The weather report had said it was supposed to rain later in the morning, but he wished it would start sooner.

He had barely slept during the night. His thoughts had just continually raced. He was filled with fear and anger. Although the fear of going to prison overcame the anger he felt towards Harold Shaw. All he kept thinking about were the nights he spent in jail. He spent those nights lying in the bottom bunk in a tiny cage. In the top bunk was a man awaiting trial for attempted murder.

Ryan tried talking to him a couple times because the silence in their cell drove him crazy, but the man never said anything. The two men in the next cell told Ryan not to bother and he wanted to listen to them, but there had to be something inside of his cellmate. Eventually he would say something.

The man didn't even look like a criminal. He was skinny and frail. He only had one tattoo on his back, but it wasn't a tattoo of a flaming skull or the grim reaper. Across his left shoulder blade was a quote that said, "'I have never been hurt by what I have not said.' – Calvin Coolidge." It was written in beautiful script. Ryan couldn't understand why of all the people in this world to quote, someone would permanently engrave the words of Calvin Coolidge on their back.

Ryan spent the days thinking or reading. His friend Matt had come to see him and brought books for Ryan to read as he had asked him to. Matt was a good friend and he and Ryan never hesitated to help each other when they needed it.

One day while Ryan was reading, his cellmate started to tap his fingers on the metal post holding up his bunk. After fifteen minutes or so, it started to irritate Ryan like an itch inside of his head that couldn't be scratched. Ryan was frustrated and annoyed. He put his feet on the floor, stood up, and glared through the rails of the man's bed at him.

"Would you like something to read?"

The man came down from the top bunk and looked Ryan in the eyes.

"I have a couple books here if you would like to read one."

The man took a book from Ryan's hand without removing his stare. He placed the book on his bunk and began to climb back up.

"You could at least say 'Thank you,' Asshole."

The man jumped back down to the floor and punched Ryan in the stomach. Ryan threw a punch back that landed on the man's face. Then he plunged the next punch into the man's stomach right before he hit him once more in the face causing the man to fall backwards. Ryan instantly regretted allowing himself to get to that boiling point.

He stepped back as far as he could before hitting the cell wall. He took a deep breath and then walked over to help the man get up from the floor. Ryan didn't say anything. He simply extended his hand, but the man wouldn't take it and got up on his own.

They stood there face-to-face and the man gave Ryan a cold and angry stare. Then the man's face contorted from angry to crazy. He opened his eyes so wide that they were mostly white. Then he closed them, shook his head back and forth as if he were having a seizure and threw his mouth open. Ryan looked in his mouth. The man didn't have a tongue. It had been cut out. It was the most horrifying thing he had ever seen.

Ryan didn't know what to say and didn't realize at first that he had even begun to speak until he heard his own voice just saying over and over, "I'm sorry. I'm sorry, Man. I'm sorry."

The man climbed up onto his bunk, lied down, and opened the book. Ryan returned back to his own bunk feeling nauseated. He didn't go back to reading. He just rolled over and stared at the wall. He didn't sleep that night. He just laid there for hours wishing for sleep.

It was the following day that Ryan found himself signing release papers. The prison guard wouldn't say who had posted Ryan's bail. Ryan was thankful though. He swore to himself that there wasn't anything he wouldn't do to repay the favor to whoever had given him his freedom.

The sun faded from the bedroom as clouds rolled over the sky outside. Ryan lied there thinking of how much he had meant that promise until yesterday morning when he had met Harold Shaw. He would have never dreamt that the man who gave him his freedom was the same man who took it away in the first place. He would also not have believed how Shaw would request that the favor be returned. He wondered if he could actually do it.

He tried to clear his mind of all of it. He tried to forget every one of the thoughts that had kept him up all night, but then Nicolette came to mind. She had a sweet and innocent smile. Her long hair danced in the ocean air. The thought of her made him feel peaceful, although not peaceful enough to go back to sleep. Ryan got up and went to the kitchen. He put on a pot of coffee. He had work to get done that day and figured he had better get started.

Chapter 6

Nicolette walked into the bathroom and looked at the circles under her eyes in the mirror above the sink. Lack of sleep was not flattering to her. She splashed cold water on her face. *It's been since Christmas since I had one of those nightmares. They better not start again. It was most likely just a onetime thing. Maybe it was because I met Ryan last night. Maybe part of me DID like him? Or maybe I'll just chalk it up to what Caitlyn said on the beach? Yep, that works.* Nicolette dried her face on a nearby hanging towel, walked out, and closed the bathroom door behind her.

The family couldn't go to the beach that day

because it rained all day with occasional thunderstorms. Nicolette, her mom, her sisters, and the kids all went to the mall about twenty-five minutes away on the mainland. Nicolette got herself an e-reader, so that she could read easily up in the attic or on the beach without having a buy a bunch of paperback books. Even though she worked as a teacher and was off for the summer, she had plenty of money in her savings account.

Almost everyone in her family worked in education as a teacher, college professor, or guidance counselor. The only one who didn't was Jerry. Fortunately though he worked for a sales company who would let him work temporarily in the Atlantic County territory and work from his lap top at the shore house. Even though he was a smart businessman, work had been steadily slowing down. The men above him and in charge of the company were running it into the ground. It had gotten bad enough that Jerry only needed to work for an hour or two on the days he worked from home.

Nicolette was looking forward to getting back to the house to set up her new e-reader and the kids were ready for their naps, so they packed up the car and headed back to the beach house. The mall was a nice distraction and all of the kids were really cute riding on the little train ride in the center court. Nicolette took their pictures and they all smiled and waved as they went by. It was a fun day, which was one of the reasons Nicolette was thankful for the rain.

Another reason was that she wouldn't have to

make the decision of whether or not she was going to walk on the beach after dinner that night. She loved to take her walks, but she wasn't sure if she wanted to chance running into Ryan again. Her first instinct was to avoid the situation completely. Luckily, the rain made that easy to do and for at least one night she didn't have to worry about it.

Everyone in the house agreed it wasn't fair for their mom to have to cook dinner every night, so everyone took turns cooking while they all visited. That night was Frank and Lisa's turn, but Frank wasn't much help in the kitchen. Nicolette went in to offer Lisa a hand so she didn't have to cook by herself.

"Thanks Nick, I appreciate it. Would you mind sitting at the table and chopping the vegetables?"

"Sure, no problem."

"You were gone for a while last night. Was everything ok? Frank said you spent that time sitting on the beach by yourself until he went looking for you. And it must have taken him a while to find you because he was gone for an hour."

"He found me almost right away I think. But then we walked up to 4th and got some ice cream."

"Ah, he neglected to mention that part. I've been on his case about us eating healthier lately. If he was going to cheat though, he could have brought me back some." Lisa said with a laugh.

"Sorry about that, Lise. Next time you and I can

go and we'll leave Frank at home."

"Deal."

"I just walked down to the beach to clear my head, but I wasn't alone the whole time. I didn't tell Frank though because I wasn't sure what to think of it at first."

"Really? Why? Who were you with?"

Nicolette proceeded to tell Lisa how she had met Ryan after he was knocked over by a wave. Then Nicolette told her how they sat there talking for a little bit and Lisa would interrupt with the occasional question.

"Was he cute?"

"I'm not really interested in meeting anyone right now."

"That wasn't what I asked, Nick. I asked if he was cute."

Nicolette continued chopping the vegetables and after a minute said, "Yes, he was very handsome."

"Who was very handsome?" Stephanie asked as she came breezing into the kitchen.

"The man Nicolette met on the beach last night."

"No wonder you were gone for so long." Stephanie said.

"It wasn't like that. He fell in the water, we had

a good laugh, and we talked for a little bit. That's all."

"But isn't that the closest thing you've had to a date in like a year?" Stephanie asked as she sat down at the table and started to peel potatoes.

"Yeah it is. I haven't been out with anyone since I went to dinner with that guy last year. But you guys, after what I did to Derrick, it's hard for me to date anyone."

Both Stephanie and Lisa stopped dead in what they were doing and turned to look at Nicolette. Lisa was the first to correct her.

"Nicolette, YOU didn't do anything to Derrick. Derrick made his own decisions and his own choices." Lisa told her just before Stephanie chimed in.

"She's absolutely right."

Believe me. I'm trying to move past it. Don't you think I want to date men and fall in love? Every time I start to feel anything for any guy, even the slightest bit of attraction, something inside me panics. I can't control it."

Lisa turned away from the stove towards Nicolette. "You have to keep trying. And this guy seems nice and you said he is handsome, so why don't you try to run into him again? Which direction did he walk in when he left?"

"He walked south along the beach and then he suddenly disappeared. It was kind of weird. But I'm not going to go looking for him, Lisa."

"I didn't mean that, I just meant that when you take your next after dinner walk on the beach, maybe walk south."

"I think you should too, Nicky. I mean, Lisa and I aren't saying you have to date this guy or fall in love with him, but maybe you could be friends with him and be able to get to a place where you can be comfortable around men again."

"So you both think I should use this guy for dating practice? That sounds a little less than healthy." Nicolette kind of snickered as she said it.

"Essentially yes, but the way we said it sounded better. Plus, it's better than just letting the problem continue. By the way, those vegetables aren't chopping themselves."

"Well, I promise I'll think about it. I can't go tonight anyway because it's raining, so it will have to wait until tomorrow."

Nicolette woke up the next day to a beautiful Sunday morning. After breakfast, the family spent the day on the beach. The hours they were there only felt like minutes to Nicolette because she kept dozing off on her beach blanket under the umbrella. She hadn't slept well again. She woke up around midnight after having another nightmare. She tossed and turned for most of the night after that.

It was around four o'clock in the afternoon when Stephanie woke Nicolette up as she was gathering the kids' beach toys out of the sand to take back to the house. Everyone else had already gone back to wash up for dinner. Nicolette got up and helped Stephanie take the toys, umbrella, and chairs back. She took a nice cool shower before dinner.

That night it was Jerry's turn to cook. He was an excellent cook, but Nicolette sat in her chair and pushed the food around her plate. She couldn't even bring herself to eat the small portions she had taken. She looked like one of the children, all of whom were moving their food around on their own plates to make it look like they ate their vegetables. She was still questioning whether or not she would walk to the beach after dinner because on that clear night, she had no excuse not to.

Nicolette excused herself, took her plate into the kitchen, and then went up to the attic.

"Pssst… Hey." Lisa'a head peeked up through the open trap door.

"Hey Lise, you can come up."

"That's ok, I just figured if you were getting changed to go for a walk that you could wear those shorts over there with your red embroidered tank top and a tie a light jacket around your waist in case it gets cold."

"I'm just going for a walk. There is no chance he'll be there again. I don't even think I want him to be. And even if he is there, I'm not going to be anymore than friends with this guy."

"I know. I know. But just humor your buttinski sister-in-law and wear these." She lifted her arm up and placed a pair of silver earrings in front of her on the floor by the opening. Then she disappeared down the rickety wooden ladder.

"Thank you."

Somehow Nicolette managed to sneak out of the house without being seen by anyone else. She walked down 3rd Street, through the dunes, and on to the beach. She had planned on following Lisa's advice and walking south down the beach, but something was telling her to go north. Maybe she was just set in that routine. Maybe she was just letting her anxiety cloud her decision.

Chapter 7

Ryan woke up on Sunday morning exhausted from not only tossing and turning during the night, but also from the work he got done around the house on the rainy day before. When Ryan had asked Matt if he could borrow the house for the week, Matt asked if Ryan would mind putting attachments above and below all of the outside windows and porch. They formed a top and bottom frame for wooden boards to fit into for hurricane protection, which Ryan also got while he was at the hardware store.

Matt would have an easy time boarding up the windows if a hurricane threatened to hit. Matt and

Ryan had been meaning to do it ever since Hurricane Gretchen came through at the end of the previous summer. The storm was so bad that the island was evacuated. It was an easy enough job for Ryan to do by himself and he was glad to be doing something to repay Matt for letting him stay at the house. It also gave him something to do on the rainy day.

No matter what Ryan did though, it didn't distract his mind from meeting Nicolette the night before. Part of him really wanted to see her again, but he also knew it wouldn't be a good idea. He was going to go to jail if he didn't do what Shaw had asked of him. However, he didn't know how much he could even trust Shaw, so even if he did what Shaw asked him to do, there was the possibility that things could still end up very badly for Ryan. In either scenario, getting involved with Nicolette would only make things more complicated.

Sunday was a beautiful day and Ryan went down to the beach to enjoy it. There were extra beach chairs and beach towels at the house, so he took one of each and walked to the entrance of the beach at the end of 6th Street. He lied in the sun and went swimming in the ocean.

It was relaxing, but it was also lonely being there by himself. He hadn't thought that it would be, since he had gotten used to being on his own. The more he thought about it though, he realized that the last time he had come to the shore, his dad had been with him. It was the year they found out he was sick. Being lonely made the decision as to whether or not he should walk to the beach again that night much more difficult. As much as he knew it wouldn't be a good idea to see Nicolette again, he just as much wanted to see her.

Chapter 8

That night after dinner, there was no one else on the beach. Nicolette was by herself, which she usually preferred. Although she caught herself looking up and down the beach several times and she realized that she was a little disappointed. She sat down in the sand and put her sandals next to her.

There had only been a slight chance that he would be there. She didn't even know how long he was staying at the shore. *He might have gone home. Plus, a couple of hours ago, I was back and forth as to whether I even wanted him to be here.* She watched the sun begin to set over the bay, but she became restless. She got up and walked over to where the last bit of waves quickly slid over the smooth sand so that the water would wash over her feet.

She loved the water. Even when her family spent days on the beach, she couldn't be out of the water for more than an hour at a time. She even went swimming earlier that day in between dozing off under the umbrella. She wasn't going to swim that night, but she did walk in another few feet so that the waves almost reached her knees.

"Watch out for rogue tidal waves."

The voice that suddenly came from the beach made her jump. She spun around and saw Ryan standing in the sand just out of reach from the foam.

"You scared me!" She yelled to him.

"Sorry about that." He laughed.

"Yeah right. You don't look sorry. I notice that you're keeping a safe distance from the water this evening."

"You're right about that."

She walked a few steps in toward him, but then stopped where the water was ankle deep. "So at least now I know that if I want you to keep your distance, I just have to stand out here, right?" She laughed.

"Or you could tell me to go away. That would be much easier."

"No, you don't have to go away. And I'll come

out of the water so you don't get scared."

"I'm not scared. It's just that after the other night I have a new respect for the strength of the under-tow at low tide."

"Well then you can respectfully stay there and I'll come out of the water."

She walked past where he was standing in the wet, muddy sand and plopped down by her shoes in the fluffy white sand on the beach.

"Was your family driving you crazy again tonight?"

"No, I just felt like going for a walk. I really like the beach at night."

"I noticed." He stood and pointed to the sand about two feet away from her and asked, "If I sit here, is this a safe enough distance or will you have to go back in the ocean again?"

"Right there is ok for now." And then she realized that it actually was ok. Her stomach tightened slightly, but not like it had other times. Maybe it was possible for her to be friends with this man. He was easy to joke with and talk to.

That night they sat there for two hours just talking about anything and everything. He told her that he worked in construction. She told him about her job and how she liked teaching high school.

"I don't think I would have learned anything in your class if you were a teacher in my high school."

"Gee, thanks."

"No, I meant that as a compliment. I wouldn't have been able to pay attention to what I should have been learning. Going through puberty is tough enough without having young, beautiful teachers."

"Maybe that's why some of the boys in my class got bad grades… and one or two girls too. I knew it was a mistake to teach in a see-through top and a wonder bra," she said sarcastically.

"Next year wear a lot of layers, you'll see a huge improvement in their grades."

"Even though I doubt that's a problem for my students, I'll give it a try."

He's so fun to talk to and joke with. Real life doesn't seem so serious when we're hanging out. I can't believe we talked for over two hours tonight. And I can't believe we've only met twice. These were just some of the thoughts that went through her head as she lied in bed that night. She was actually happy for the first time in so long. She drifted off to sleep, but images began to sweep her mind as another nightmare began.

Nicolette was sitting in a chair in the prison's visiting room. She stared at the glass partition in front of her. There was no one on the other side. She looked next to her on both sides. Every other chair was occupied by someone talking into a phone to a loved one on the other side of the glass. Everyone was telling whoever they were talking to that they loved them and they missed them. Some of them were holding up photographs to the glass. Nicolette turned back to face her own partition, but it was smeared with blood. She stood and leaned over trying to wipe it off, but it was on the other side. She picked up the black phone next to her.

"I can't see you. You have to wipe the blood off. You have to wipe it off! I can't see you!"

A deep, raspy voice came through the phone. "You can't see me because I'm not coming."

Nicolette's eyes blinked open in bed. She could barely see in the dark attic, only a little bit of moonlight came in the small porthole window. She slept with a portable fan on, since the attic wasn't completely air conditioned. Her face, pillow, and t-shirt were tear and sweat stained and cold from the air blowing lightly on the moisture.

She had woken up from her nightmare at four-thirty in the morning and hadn't been able to fall back to sleep. Once again, that day she dozed off lying on a large blanket on the beach. Frank and Jerry had all of the kids down by the water building a giant sand castle, so it was easier than usual to drift off.

Chapter 9

Ryan got up that same morning at four o'clock. He brushed his teeth, put on deodorant and clean clothes, and was in his truck by four fifteen. He drove off of the island and got onto the highway. By six-thirty he was in Northeast Philadelphia. Ryan found the street he had only been to once before and parked his truck in the long driveway.

He walked up the winding brick walkway and knocked on the door. A woman came to the door in her robe.

"Can I help you?"

"I'm looking for Mr. Shaw."

"Do you know what time it is?"

As she asked this, Shaw appeared behind her. "Gina, go and put some coffee on in the kitchen. I'll be right there."

The woman didn't question what he said. She just turned and walked through the foyer to the hallway. Ryan lost sight of her almost immediately because Shaw almost pushed him over as he quickly came out of the front door, closing it behind him.

"Westin, what the hell are you doing here? I gave you strict instructions to call me at the number I gave you on Wednesday."

"I'm here to give you my answer today. I'm not going to do it."

Shaw pursed his lips and then put his hand in his chin with his index finger over his mouth. Deep in thought, he walked past Ryan down the walkway toward Ryan's truck. Once he reached the driveway he turned to Ryan. "Westin, I have made you an incredibly generous offer. My offer still stands of course because I meant what I said. It's obvious though, that you need a little more motivation."

"I don't need motivation for something I'm not going to do." Ryan said firmly.

Shaw gave him a regretful look. "I should apologize to you. When I made this proposition to you, there was something I didn't tell you."

"What didn't you tell me?"

"I only kept it from you because I didn't want to dredge up any painful memories. I know how hard it must have been losing your father so suddenly."

"Don't pretend like you give a damn about me."

"Fine. Do you want to know who that person is that was in the file I showed you? It was the other person in the car that killed your father."

"There were two people in the car? I thought the driver was the only one."

"No. There was a driver and another person in the passenger seat. The driver was taking another person home; a person who should have recognized that the driver was too drunk to get behind the wheel; the same person in the file I showed you."

Ryan stood there not knowing how to respond. His confusion started to blend with anger. He couldn't move.

Shaw took Ryan by the arm and walked him to his truck like a child being pulled to his room by an angry parent after he did something bad. "Westin, I'm going to pretend that you didn't come here this morning. You are going to get into your truck and leave. The next time I speak to you will be on Wednesday when you call me at the number I gave you. You will not show up here again."

Shaw left Ryan standing by the driver's side door of his truck and turned and walked back to the house. Ryan got into his truck and started his drive back to the shore. As he drove back down the highway he thought about the night of his father's accident: the phone call, the hospital, Officer Angeloni, Dr. Walters, and the nurse. None of them had mentioned that there had been a second person in the car.

Ryan returned to the beach house around ten o'clock that morning. He went to the little diner on the main drag before going to the beach for a little while. He felt lost. He didn't know what to do and Shaw's words continually echoed through his mind. He had told Nicolette he would meet her at the beach that night. He wanted to see her. After meeting with Shaw that morning, he *needed* to see her.

Chapter 10

Once Nicolette got home from the beach and took a shower, she felt completely refreshed. While she was getting dressed and ready in the attic before dinner, she heard footsteps on the old, creaky ladder. Stephanie's head popped up through the opening in the floor.

"Can we come up?"

"We who?" Nicolette laughed.

"Me, Lisa, and Marie."

"Sure, come on up."

"So what happened last night?" Lisa asked.

"Did you see that guy again? What's his name?"

"Ryan. And yes, I ran into him again on the beach."

"How did it go?"

"It was a lot of fun actually. We just sat and talked for a while and it was really nice."

Marie made a face as she said, "Nice? My in-laws are 'nice.' You have to give us something better than that."

"Well, we planned to meet again tonight, but that's all I got for you. I'm sorry to disappoint, but we're just going to be friends."

Stephanie looked from Marie to Lisa, and then back to Nicolette before she asked, "Then why are you putting on makeup?"

"I don't know."

"I think you like him and you just won't admit it to yourself." Marie said.

"And it's ok if you do. It's a good thing, not something to get upset over." Lisa chimed in.

"Plus, it's about time you let go of all that crap with Derrick anyway. I mean come on, get over it already."

Stephanie shot Marie a stern look. "You know, you can go back downstairs anytime you want

Marie. Saying things like that isn't helpful."

"Excuse me for trying to give my sister some advice. And I'm sorry, but it needed to be said." Marie got up, climbed through the hole in the floor, and carefully went down the ladder.

Nicolette dabbed at her eye with a tissue to keep her freshly applied mascara from running. Lisa went over and squatted next to Nicolette. She put her hand on her knee. "Please don't be upset. You know not to listen to her."

"No, she's right. I need to move on. I don't know why I'm having such a hard time doing it though. I've even started having nightmares again."

Stephanie went over and put her arm around Nicolette and said, "You don't *need* to do anything. What you should do though is focus on being happy now. Go down to the beach tonight and having fun with Ryan. And if you just want to be friends with him, there's nothing wrong with that."

Nicolette thought about the conversation she had with her sisters as she walked down to the beach after dinner. She walked north to the point and Ryan was there waiting for her in the same spot. He was sitting on a blanket looking out over the water. Nicolette walked over and joined him. They started talking, but something about him seemed different that night. He was distracted somehow or Nicolette wondered if something was on his mind. Although, she didn't want to specifically ask, so she moved the conversation in a different direction.

Nicolette asked, "If you love the shore so much, why did you say you haven't come here in a few years?"

"From the time I was about five years old, my dad used to bring me here for a week every summer. We would go fishing every day. Then on some days we would go crabbing and cook all of the crabs we caught and have a feast that night. My dad had this great recipe for cooking them. They would be nice a spicy and make our hands all messy."

"That sounds like fun. Your dad sounds like a great guy."

"He was. Even as I got older, we still always came here for one week every year. The last year that we did it was the year he got sick. We came in the summer and he was diagnosed with cancer in the fall. He died shortly after. I haven't been back here since then."

"I can see why it would be tough for you to come here." Nicolette said relieved that he was more talkative now. She wondered if that had been what was bothering him.

"Plus, it felt like no one understood what I was going through. My friends told me counseling would help or even group therapy. People even gave me books on how to deal with losing a loved one, but I just used them for kindling in the fire pit in my back yard."

"I'm sure everyone told you things like, 'time will heal your pain,' and 'things will get better eventually.'"

"Yeah, like that just makes everything better."

"I know how you feel."

"Yeah, people told me that too, but how could anyone know what it feels like."

"No, I mean me… I actually know how you feel. I know what it's like to lose someone very close to you."

"Who did you lose?"

"My boyfriend."

Chapter 11

Ryan sat there and listened intently as Nicolette began to tell him how she had lost her boyfriend.

"I haven't spoken to anyone about it since it happened, except to my brother Frank and my sister-in-law Lisa. The rest of the family tries to be supportive, but they've just got too many other things going on and I'm not as close with my other siblings."

"How did he die?"

"I guess you could call it suicide, but it all started when we were in a car accident. It's a long story and I'm not sure how to explain it."

"Start from the beginning." He seemed more like he was insisting, rather than encouraging her to tell him what happened, which made Nicolette hesitate a little.

"His name was Derrick. Three years ago we were in a car accident. We were coming home from a party at his friend's house and he was driving us to my apartment. I had a lot to drink that night and couldn't drive. He had been drinking too, but insisted he was perfectly fine to drive home. I tried to tell him that we should call a cab, but he just kept saying he was fine and that I worry too much. We started driving, but the drive is a blur to me now. I remember seeing the red traffic light though. Derrick didn't see that the light was red and went through it. I don't remember what happened after that, but the witnesses told the police that a man happened to be pulling out onto the road from a parking lot just after the light. They said he probably assumed our car was going to stop at the light, but that they didn't remember even seeing our brake lights come on at all." Ryan felt his eyes begin to water, but luckily he didn't cry as Nicolette told him the story.

It was his father whom Nicolette and Derrick had hit. It was shortly after the point Nicolette was at in her story that Ryan received the phone call. He was getting almost a first-hand account of what happened the night his father died. Anger churned in his stomach. If Derrick hadn't driven that night, if he would have listened to Nicolette, Ryan would have had another year with his father or more. It was with that thought that Ryan realized that Nicolette wasn't to blame for what happened. Shaw was wrong. And Ryan hated Shaw even more for trying to use his father's accident in trying to manipulate him. Ryan needed to hear the whole story. He needed her to tell him the rest, so he tried to keep her talking about it.

"What happened to him?"

"What happened to Derrick or the man in the other car?"

"Well, both I guess." He said, even though Ryan knew all too well what happened to the other man.

"Our car, or Derrick's car I should say, slammed into his truck and it flew forward into the metal pole of a street light. So many cops came along with ambulances. Derrick was unconscious. I had a gash in my side, a sprained knee, and a lot of bumps and bruises. Our airbags had gone off luckily. The other man's truck was older. I don't know what kind, but his airbag didn't go off when he hit the pole. He was conscious though when they put him into the ambulance. Since I wasn't badly hurt, they were able to get me out of the car and into an ambulance faster than Derrick and the other man, so I arrived to the hospital first. They pushed me through the automatic doors, past the waiting room, and left me in my stretcher in the hallway, just through the double doors of Our Lady of Lourdes emergency room. Then all of the other EMTs came rushing in. They wheeled the man past me. He was covered in a blood stained sheet. Then two more EMTs rushed Derrick by me. Derrick survived the accident. The other man didn't."

Ryan watched tears roll down Nicolette's face. He couldn't stand seeing women cry. He was wearing a green long-sleeved cotton shirt and cargo shorts. He pulled his hand into his sleeve and used the cuff of it to wipe her tears.

"Sorry, I don't have any tissues."

"Thank you."

"So obviously you were ok after the accident. But what happened to Derrick?"

"Physically Derrick was fine after the accident. It was the combination of the alcohol and the shock of the accident that made him pass out. Other than that, he only had minor cuts from the glass of the windshield. The following morning he was released from the hospital and taken to jail. I found out during his initial hearing that it was his third DUI in five years. He never told me about any of them. He hadn't suffered any penalties for them either because his father is a high powered district attorney in Philadelphia, so naturally he has a lot of connections."

Ryan knew she was talking about Harold Shaw. Shaw was Derrick's father that son-of-a-bitch. His anger and hatred toward Shaw burned through him. "I hate when bad people are given so much power." He said as he clenched his jaw.

"He is a very corrupt man, but his record is spotless and very few people will try to cross him. Although he couldn't sweep what Derrick did under the rug because someone had been killed. Derrick was sentenced to five years in jail for manslaughter in addition to drinking and driving. After he was sentenced, I only went one time to visit him. I told him that it would be the only time I would come to prison to see him. He begged me to not give up on him and that his father would make sure he was released much sooner than his sentence."

"That's a lot to ask of someone, especially someone you love."

"Yes it is. He also said that even if I didn't love him anymore or want to stay with someone who was in prison, I was the only person he really cared about and that he needed me as a friend. He said he wouldn't survive in that place if he couldn't see my face or hear my voice. He asked me to come and visit him, if only once a month, every two months, or even every six months. I really did love him, but I told him that I would never come back to visit him. He lied to me, he almost got me killed, and he killed an innocent person. I told him that I wasn't ever coming back."

"That must have been really hard for you."

"It was. It killed me to do it. Even though I hadn't forgiven him, I missed him so much and I still loved him. I went back about a month later to visit him, but when I got there they shuffled me into an office. One of the administrators told me he was dead. They told me that he had been killed by a fellow inmate two days before that, but they weren't able to divulge any more information than that."

"But you said he committed suicide?"

"Derrick's father was actually the one to find out that it was an alleged suicide. It was officially ruled as a murder, but through whatever connections he has, Derrick's father was able to find out that Derrick was very depressed and had been provoking the inmate for a couple weeks. The inmate was apparently twice Derrick's size and a violent offender. Derrick started the fight, but only got in a few punches before the other man broke his neck. It happened before the guards could intervene."

"I'm so sorry, Nicolette. That is terrible." Ryan tried to sound as sincere as possible. He was honestly sorry for what Nicolette went through, but he wasn't sorry that Derrick was killed.

"It's my fault that he's dead. His whole family blamed me, especially his father. They said I should have never let him get behind the wheel or that I should have realized he was too drunk to drive and called a cab. And it's all true. Plus, I didn't have to drink that night and then I could have driven home."

"You can't do that to yourself."

"If I hadn't been so angry on the day I visited him and told him that I wouldn't be back maybe he wouldn't have been so depressed."

Ryan sat a thought about it. He remembered what he had gone through in jail. It was enough to depress anyone. "You can't blame yourself for what happened to him, especially while he was in prison. Plus, if he was as depressed as his father said then he probably could have gotten help while he was in there. Not to mention the fact that he made the choice to drink and drive."

"I should have insisted on calling a cab or something."

"No, *he* should have called a cab, but he didn't. He wouldn't listen when you tried to tell him to either. He got behind the wheel of a car, which he had gotten caught doing two times before when you had absolutely nothing to do with it. Who knows how many times he had done it *without* getting caught?"

Nicolette sat and thought for a few minutes about what Ryan said. He was right. The same thoughts had gone through her mind before as well.

"I guess."

"You're a good person."

"I'm sure that man's family doesn't think so. I still get nightmares thinking about the whole thing and about that man. He didn't do anything wrong and he still had so much of his life ahead of him. I don't even know if he had a family. I'm sure he did, but the only thing I ever found out about him was that he was only sixty-four years old. I don't even know his name."

"Ed."

Nicolette did a double take and then stared at Ryan with a shocked and questioning look. "What did you say?"

Ryan hadn't meant to say it. It had come out of

his mouth so naturally without him even realizing it. He sat and thought for a minute. Since it had been said at that point, he decided to tell her the rest. "His name was Ed. He didn't have much family, only one son."

"How could you possibly know that?"

"He was my father. His name was Ed Westin."

"But you just told me a little while ago that your father died from cancer."

"I didn't say he died from cancer. I said that he was diagnosed with cancer and died shortly after that. But he died in a car accident when he was hit by a drunk driver."

"That's not possible. That is the most ridiculous coincidence I have ever heard, there is no way that it's true. Why would you lie to me? I'm sitting here telling you about the worst thing that has ever happened to me and you're going to make up some wild story about how it involves you? That's sick!"

Nicolette stood up to leave. She picked up her sandals and turned to storm off.

"It was a red truck." As Ryan said this, Nicolette froze.

She stood silently with her back to him for a minute or so before she replied. "A lot of trucks are red."

"The accident happened at the 7-11 on Route 130. The man pulled out of a 7-11 parking lot."

Ryan watched as Nicolette slowly turned back around. Even on the dark beach, Ryan could tell how hard she was beginning to cry. She dropped her sandals at her side and covered her face with her hands. "Yes he did."

"I know. They told me about the accident when I arrived at the hospital. But I never knew who had been in the other car until today."

"Ryan, I'm so sorry. I'm so so sorry. I can't believe... I don't know... I wish I could go back." She was sobbing too hard to form complete sentences.

Ryan got up, walked over to her and hugged her. "It wasn't your fault. Please don't cry."

"But if it weren't for me, you would still have your father."

"No, I really wouldn't. You're wrong about that."

"What do you mean?"

"If I tell you, will you sit back down and promise to stop crying?" Ryan looked down at her and half smiled. He wiped her tears again with his sleeve.

"I'll sit back down, but I can't make any promises." She said trying to force a smile as well.

Nicolette was able to stop crying as Ryan explained everything to her about his father. He told her that he had been diagnosed with pancreatic cancer and was refusing treatment. He told her about the day of his doctor's appointment and that he told Ryan he wasn't going to want any help.

"To tell you the truth, a car accident is probably how my dad would have rather went. Instead of the cancer slowly eating away at him over the course of one or two years, he was only in pain for less than an hour."

"It probably doesn't make you feel any better, but the police and ambulances got there really fast. It couldn't even have been as long as an hour that he was in pain."

"My father would have hated every minute of being sick, especially if he stopped being able to do things for himself. That would have not only killed him, but it would have also humiliated him first."

He sat there for twenty minutes or so talking about his dad. He told her how stubborn he was and that he was too proud to ask for help with anything. Then he spent the next half hour telling her the funny stories he remembered about his dad.

Ryan told Nicolette about the time when he was eleven and his dad took him crabbing. "We went out onto the boat, but we forgot to bring the big cooler with us. We only had a small one that we had left on the boat from before. Well naturally, since we only had a small cooler, we started catching crabs by the dozens. That little cooler was almost overflowing. Well, one of those little guys managed to crawl out of it, but we didn't notice. He grabbed my dad's little toe with its claw and wouldn't let go. My dad tried to get it off, but he fell right over the edge of the boat into the ocean!"

Ryan could tell that Nicolette was feeling better. And if she wasn't enjoying his stories about his dad, she was really good at pretending. They sat in silence for a moment as he tried to think of another.

"I'm sure with all of those brothers and sisters that you have some funny stories of your own."

"I definitely do, but if I start telling you stories about my family, we may be here all night."

She lifted her hand and tucked a few stray strands of his sandy blonde hair behind his ear. Her fingertips felt soft as they brushed against his face and ear. He wanted to kiss her, but he knew he shouldn't.

Chapter 12

Things had gone too far too quickly. He was sinking in a situation that was like quick sand. The more he did, the more it sucked him under. Ryan stayed perfectly still and waited for her to pull her hand back. Instead of pulling back, she leaned in and gently kissed his lips. She leaned back and looked into his eyes. She had the most beautiful green eyes.

He didn't know what to do. She was waiting for his reaction. His heart was beating so fast that he felt short of breath and his mind clouded over. For a brief moment he forgot why he shouldn't kiss her. He pushed his hand through his tear-stained sleeve so that he could hold her face in his hands. He pulled her to him and kissed her. It was a long, slow, romantic kiss that made time stand still.

It felt so good to give in to what he had been wanting, but thought he should never get. "I've wanted to do that since the first time I saw you sitting on the beach a few nights ago."

"Then do it again."

He pulled her in closely and this time kissed her passionately. They couldn't feel the cool ocean wind anymore, just the heat radiating from their bodies into each other. Ryan leaned her back and gently cradled her head as he lied her down on the blanket. Then Nicolette slid one arm underneath his side. They wrapped each other in their arms and Ryan shifted his weight, overcoming hers, and kissed her again.

After a few minutes he pulled back, propped himself up on his elbow, and looked down at her. She pulled her arm back slowly from around his back caressing it with her hand as she did. Then she traced the outline of his chest over his t-shirt before she put it on the ground as she propped herself on her side using her elbow as well.

"I guess now it's my turn to say thank you." Nicolette told him.

"Oh yeah, why is that?"

"Because I have never been kissed like that."

"I find that hard to believe. You're too beautiful not to be kissed like that."

"Then why did you stop?"

Ryan didn't know how to start. He didn't know how to tell her the truth, so instead he took the easy way out. "I just don't want to rush anything. I've never even taken you on a real date. Why don't you come over for dinner tomorrow night? I can cook… and by cook, I mean order some very nice take out."

Nicolette laughed. "That sounds nice. I can bring a movie over to watch if you want?"

"Sure that sounds great. I'm staying on 6th Street, number 428. I'm on the second block from the beach." Ryan said as he stood up and reached down to help Nicolette up."

"What time should I come over?"

He didn't have anything to do the next day, but he was still having trouble thinking clearly. "Umm… Come over around 6:30."

Nicolette helped him fold up the blanket and they walked together to the 3rd Street pathway to the beach. They both stopped and Ryan put his arms around her. He bent down and kissed her goodnight.

"I'll see you tomorrow."

"Goodnight."

Ryan's mind started racing again as he walked toward 6th Street. He had to do something. What he was doing wasn't fair to her. He cared about her so much, but no matter what decision he made, no matter what he told Shaw, things were only going to keep getting worse for both him and Nicolette.

Chapter 13

When Nicolette walked up to the house, it was completely dark except for the kitchen light, but she heard laughter coming from inside. She walked around the house to go in the back door. She walked up the steps and through the porch door into the small washroom. Through the glass in the main door leading to the kitchen, she could see her brothers Jerry and Frank and her brothers-in-law Pete and Joe all sitting around the table playing poker. She looked at her watch. It was 1:00am and she was going to hear about it in the next two seconds.

She opened the door and walked into the kitchen. She took one step through the door and hit a wall of cigar smoke and the smell of beer.

"Well, look who it is!"

"And where were you until all hours of the night?"

"Isn't it past your bed time, Young Lady?"

"Ha ha. Very funny, guys. And Jerry, I haven't had a bed time in seventeen years. I'm twenty nine years old." Nicolette went over to the sink and started rinsing the empty beer cans so she could put them out back in the recycling bucket. When she returned from outside, she walked back into the wall of smoke. "I don't even believe you guys are smoking in here. Are you crazy? Mom is going to kill you!" Nicolette walked over and opened the window over the sink and brought a small fan in.

"Dad was the one who started smoking in here first anyway." Frank said.

"Dad was smoking? How much did he have to drink?"

"About five scotch and sodas... hold the sodas."

"Mom is going to be so pissed when she wakes up tomorrow."

"Mom is pissed right now." Their mother said as she walked into the kitchen with her hands on her hips. "You put those cigars out right now or you take them outside. I don't want my grandbabies breathing that shit in while they're trying to eat breakfast in the morning." Her hair had been pulled up in a clip, but was disheveled. She was half asleep, but still very annoyed. "I got up to pee, but when I got out of bed I tripped over your damn father who is passed out on the floor. Just what the hell did you boys do to him anyway?"

They all looked at each other until Jerry told her, "Ma, he had a little too much scotch, so we sent him up to bed."

"And Nicolette, don't tell me you're just getting in at this hour. Where have you been? It's not safe for you to be out and about this late at night by yourself. Explain yourself, Young Lady."

"She got in a while ago, but stayed down here to watch the game since all the girls were asleep already." Frank lied.

"Plus Ma, she's twenty nine years old."

"Jerry, when I want your opinion I'll give it to you."

Their mother walked over and hugged Nicolette. "Don't you stay up too late either, especially since you don't want to be down here breathing all this stuff anyway. I love you, Sweetie pie." Then she turned and walked out of the kitchen.

In unison, all the men mimicked their mother (or mother-in-law in Pete and Joe's cases). "Good night, Shweetie Pie…"

"All of you shut up, clean up this mess, put out those damn cigars, and go to bed!" Their mother's voice echoed from the next room.

They all chuckled and went back to playing their game, so Nicolette took the opportunity to say that she was going to head up to bed too. *There's no way I'm going to be able to go to sleep now, but I don't want to stay down here and get interrogated.*

"Whoa, where do you think you're going? Sit your ass down and tell us what you've been out doing all night, since Frank was nice enough to cover for you."

Damn.

"I was down on the beach with a friend of mine."

"What's her name?" Joe asked.

"From what Stephanie told me it's not a *her*, it's a *him*." Pete replied.

"Is that who you've been with every night for the past few days?" Jerry asked.

"Yes, but he's just a friend." Nicolette told him.

"Doesn't sound like it to me." Joe laughed.

"Well it's none of your business anyway, now is it Joe?"

"Ha! She told you." Frank said.

Joe imitated the way Nicolette moved back and forth when she said something sassy, "I thought it was my business to look out for my sister-in-law."

"Well, Joe I appreciate it, but I'll be just fine."

"I hope you're not going out with him tomorrow night. Isn't it your turn to cook dinner?" Pete asked.

"Oh shit! I forgot. Can someone else switch nights with me? I'm going to his house for dinner."

"You're going to his house? Where does he live?" If it was possible, Frank's ears would have perked up like a dog's does when it hears a strange noise.

"He lives over on 6th street. And what's wrong with going to his house?"

"Why don't you have him come here for dinner?"

"Frank, are you crazy? Bring him around this family? You know how piranhas can completely devour an entire cow in like under a minute? I bet you all could beat that time."

"She does have a point. No offense, but the first time Marie brought me here to meet all of you I felt like I was being interrogated on one of those cop shows. I was ready to confess anything, even when I didn't do anything wrong." Joe said.

"That's just the initiation that we put all new people through." Jerry laughed.

"Well, this one is too new and I'm not even dating him, so I'm not bringing him over for dinner."

Frank put down his cards and gave her a serious look. "Well if you go to his house, it will send him the wrong message."

Joe picked up his beer. "Yeah it does. Bow-chicka-bow-wow."

"Grow up, Joe." She snapped.

"He's right though."

"I know what I'm doing you guys. I'm not sending any messages. I'm just going there for dinner. Frank, can you please make dinner tomorrow? Please?"

"Fine, but you have to cook on my next two turns."

"Thank you, Frank," Nicolette said as she hugged him and then left to go upstairs."Good night, guys." She said over her shoulder to the rest of them.

Frank waited until he heard the upstairs door shut before he turned his attention back to his brothers, "I don't have a good feeling about this guy she's seeing."

"Have you met him?"

"No, but…"

"Then how could you possibly feel anything about him?" Jerry asked.

"Stephanie told me he's always been overprotective of her." Pete chimed in.

"Well, she's my little sister. I'm supposed to protect her."

"She's my little sister too," said Jerry. "And what about the twins? Aren't they our little sisters?"

"Yeah but the twins are bitches." Frank smiled and then let out a loud burp.

"You're right about that." Jerry agreed and they all laughed.

Even Joe laughed until he realized that they were talking about his wife. "Hey!"

Chapter 14

The next morning, Nicolette, Lisa, and Stephanie were sitting on the front porch drinking cups of coffee. Everyone else was in the house eating the big pancake breakfast their mother was making. Nicolette told them about the night before. At first they couldn't believe that Nicolette had told Ryan about Derrick, but they were glad to hear that it worked out for the best, instead of the whole thing scaring him off.

"I still can't believe I kissed him. I can't believe I didn't panic or even hesitate. It has been so long since I've been able to do that. I am nervous about going to his house for dinner though. Speaking of which, Lisa I hope you don't mind but I asked Frank if you guys could take my turn for dinner."

"Of course Frank and I will take your turn for dinner tonight, Nick! I'm so excited for you."

"What do you think will happen?" Stephanie asked. "Do you think you'll sleep with him? You haven't known him very long, although that never stopped me when I was in my twenties."

"Yeah, me either." Lisa agreed.

"I'm not sure. After we kissed, he kind of backed off a little. He told me he has liked me since the first time we met and I know he wanted to kiss me, but then it was like something spooked him."

"Are you that bad of a kisser?" Stephanie and Lisa both laughed.

"I didn't think so." Nicolette joined in the laughter. "Just don't tell Mom and Dad. You'll know they'll want to meet him and I don't even know what's going to happen or even what this thing is between me and him. I really thought that I was going to have the same reaction that I've had recently with any other guy, as soon as I start to feel anything I just want to run and hide. This time was so different though."

Lisa looked Nicolette in the eye. "Telling him about what you've been through is a very intimate thing to share with someone. You haven't let yourself be that vulnerable with anyone for a long time. This is a good thing that's happening. Let it happen. Just also be careful that it all isn't too much too soon."

"Uh oh." Stephanie was the first to see their mother coming towards the sliding glass door.

Their mother opened the door, stepped out onto the deck, and slid it closed behind her. "Nicolette, why didn't you tell me you were seeing someone? That's wonderful, Dear."

Nicolette looked at Stephanie and Lisa, whose expressions were almost as confused as her own. "I'm not seeing him, Mom. We're just friends."

"Well either way, you invite him to come over for dinner tonight. I would like to meet him."

"Mom, we're supposed to be going out for a bite to eat."

"Well then this will save him a little money, won't it? Plus, if he's just a friend then there should be no reason why he would mind meeting your family."

"Regardless, you know those guys are going to rake him over the coals."

Jerry opened the sliding glass door. "Ma, the pancakes on the stove are burning."

"Are your arms broken for God's sake? Flip them then!"

"You have the spatula in your hand!"

"Here, take it. I'll be right there. She handed Jerry spatula and then turned back to Nicolette. "I'll have a talk with your brothers. You tell him to come over at 5:30 sharp. He'll get to see what a good cook you are." Through the glass door behind her, the smoke alarm started to go off in the house and Jordan started to cry.

"But Mom, I'm not…"

"You tell him we'll see him at 5:30 and that we're looking forward to meeting him." Then she walked back into the house, shutting the door behind her.

Lisa looked at Stephanie and then at Nicolette. "Which one of them do you think told her?"

"I'll bet any amount of money it was your husband."

"No, not even Frank would stoop that low to keep you from doing something."

"It was probably Pete. He has such a big mouth. That's part of the reason why I married him." Stephanie said with a smirk and Lisa and Nicolette couldn't help but laugh.

"Oh my God, you're so bad. I can't believe how happy she is that she thinks I'm seeing someone."

"Ok first off, you ARE seeing him. Second, she's been as worried about you as the rest of us have."

"I don't have Ryan's phone number, so I'll have

to go to his house to ask him if he would like to come to dinner."

"You don't have his phone number? Do you even know his last name?"

Nicolette sat and thought for a moment. She actually didn't know his last name. The more she thought about it, she had never told him her last name either. *We know so much about each other. How did that never come up?*

Stephanie's eyes widened. "Nick!"

"Well, it just never came up in conversation."

"I would find out what it is before what seems more and more like a very interesting dinner."

"I will. And here's what I'll do: I'll just make sure that I cook something tonight that can be eaten quickly. I won't make any extra courses either, not even a salad. Hopefully that way we can be in and out in less than an hour. I know. I'll make tacos and Spanish rice."

"And we'll do whatever we can to make sure everything goes smoothly." Lisa added.

"Oh sure, I help her and then she makes me sleep next to Pete after he is going to put about a gallon of hot sauce on his tacos."

After breakfast, Nicolette put on her bikini and a pair of shorts, grabbed a towel, and walked down to the beach. She heard someone calling her name and turned to see Marie and Cate waving at her from about fifty yards away. They yelled over to her and told her to come and sit with them.

Nicolette walked over and spread her towel out over the hot sand next to Cate's chair and took off her flip-flops and shorts. She told them she was going to go for a swim and that she would be right back. About fifteen minutes later, she came back out of breath and collapsed onto her towel.

"How is the water today?" Marie asked.

"It feels great. You guys should go for a swim."

"Maybe later." Cate said from under her umbrella. "So we heard you're bringing a friend to dinner?"

"I'm not sure, I haven't asked him yet. I was going to go to his house to extend the invitation when I left here."

"You might want to stop at home and put on some make-up first."

Nicolette didn't feel like arguing with her. She let the comment go and simply responded with, "That's a good idea. Maybe I'll stop at home before I go over."

"Just a suggestion."

Nicolette lied down on her towel and let the sun dry her. She laid there for a little while and then asked Marie if she knew what time it was. Marie told her it was around noon, so Nicolette got up and put her shorts back on. She slipped on her flip-flops, collected her towel, and walked back to the 3rd Street beach entrance. Instead of going back to the house, she walked by it and made a left. She walked to 6th Street and looked for number 428.

The house was two stories, but narrow. It was a dark blue-gray color with white trim and had a porch in the front with an upstairs deck above it. She was nervous walking up to the front door. She knocked lightly, but didn't hear anything on the other side of the door, so she tried knocking again, this time a little louder. He's probably not home. I'll go home and shower and then stop back. *This would be much easier if I had his phone number.*

Then she heard Ryan's voice, but it wasn't coming from the other side of the door. It was coming from the side of the house. Nicolette walked across the front porch and peered around the corner. She could hear his voice a little better, but couldn't make out what he was saying and he sounded upset. She went back down the front steps, off of the porch, and walked around through the narrow side yard that was made up of gravel instead of grass. She could see that one of the windows was open and that was where Ryan's voice was coming from.

Nicolette took off her flip-flops and tip-toed in her bare feet on the stepping stones from one to the other so that her feet wouldn't crunch in the gravel. She stopped just short of the window where she could hear Ryan clearly. *He must be on the phone.*

"I told you I can't do it… I can't accept it… I understand that but… I'm willing to take the chance… Hello? Hello? Shit!"

Nicolette tip-toed back to the front of the house and put her flip-flops back on. She walked up the steps once more and tried knocking on the door again. This time she heard footsteps through the house and the front door swung open.

"Nicolette…"

"Hi Ryan, I know I'm a little early and under dressed."

"I wouldn't call six hours a *little* early, but if you want to wear that any time you come over, I'm perfectly ok with that."

"Are you ok? You look like you're flustered about something. Your face is all red."

He hesitated for a moment. "Oh I'm fine. I'm just pissed off at one of my foremen. The guy is a real pain in my ass. I would fire him, but his workers love him and they do a good job under him."

"Ok, well I didn't want to bother you. I just had a quick question."

"You're not bothering me at all. Do you want to come in?"

"I can't, my feet are all sandy. I was just on the beach."

"No kidding? I couldn't tell. There is a hose out back I think. I'll show you where it is and then you can rinse your feet off and come inside because you'll be out of excuses of why you can't."

Ryan opened the screen door and walked out onto the porch and down the steps. Nicolette trailed behind him.

"I wanted to ask you if you wanted to come over for dinner tonight. Even though I tried to tell them over and over that we're just friends, my family found out that you're the one I've been spending so much time with this week and they want to meet you. I completely understand if you don't want to, but if you don't I'll never get them off my back and I probably won't be able to come over tonight without telling them about a hundred lies…"

"That sounds great. I don't mind meeting your family."

"That's only because you haven't met them yet." She said as they reached the back yard.

Ryan unwound about three feet of hose and turned the nozzle on. "Plus, I only have a few more days of vacation left and I want to be able to spend as much of that time with you as I can."

Nicolette held out her hand to take the hose from him. And Ryan pulled it back. "Just stick out your foot, I'll do it."

"It's ok. I can clean off my own feet."

"What? You don't trust me?" He smiled.

"Honestly no, I don't. Here, give me the hose."

"Ok, fine. Here." Ryan squeezed the nozzle and let out a quick spray hitting Nicolette in the stomach.

She jumped back. "Holy shit, that's cold!"

"It is? I'm sorry. It was an accident." He said and sprayed her again.

She stepped toward him and grabbed the nozzle with her hand and tried to turn it toward him. She couldn't quite turn it all the way, but water sprayed in every direction, including all over him.

"Oh crap, that *is* cold!"

"I told you! And now I'm soaked."

"Yeah, but you're feet are clean."

As she looked down at her feet, she saw his feet take a step closer to her. She felt his hand slide over her bare wet skin around her back. His other hand dropped the hose to the ground and moved through her hair to the back of her neck as his muscular arms pulled her in close. She looked up, but closed her eyes as his lips came in to meet hers. Their mouths moved around each other, interlocking perfectly. She let herself press into him.

After a few perfect minutes, he pulled his lips back slightly and whispered, "Do you want to come in?"

"I really wish I could." She kissed him again. "But I have to go home. I have to make dinner." She pulled back a little further.

"What time should I come over?" He said right before he pulled her back in and kissed her again.

"Come over by 5:30. If you survive dinner, then we can come back here after." She said out of breath. "But right now I really have to go."

"Ok, if you really have to." His hands slid from her back to her hips and then they fell to his sides.

Nicolette picked up her flip-flops and Ryan walked her back out front.

"Oh yeah and the house is on 3rd Street. It's the white house with the red shutters, number 202, you can't miss it."

"I'll see you soon."

Nicolette stood on the tips of her toes, pecked him lightly on the lips, and then turned and walked down the front walkway leading from the porch to the sidewalk. She stopped about halfway and turned around. "I almost forgot to ask you… what's your last name?"

Ryan smiled. "Westin. Ryan Westin."

"Nicolette Carson." She smiled back at him and turned again to walk toward the street.

Ryan stood and watched her walk away until she was across the street and then he turned to go back into the house.

Chapter 15

That night Nicolette almost wore a hole in the kitchen floor walking back and forth making dinner. Lisa came in to help her and so did Marie. Stephanie and Natalie were trying to feed the kids. Mom was helping them since it was too difficult even for two people. It was easier for the family to eat in shifts with the four kids eating first, so that all the adults could sit and eat in peace at the same time a little bit later. It was also better that way since the kids didn't like tacos. They were eating baked chicken nuggets and applesauce. Maya was crying because applesauce touched one of her chicken nuggets and her mother, Natalie was trying to comfort her and cut off the contaminated piece of nugget containing the applesauce.

In the kitchen, Marie diced tomatoes and put them into bowls. Lisa chopped lettuce. They bought pre-shredded cheese, so that only needed to be put in bowls at the last minute. Nicolette had the meat simmering on the stove, the shells in the oven, and she frantically looked for little bowls to put sour cream in. She looked at the clock. 5:23. She pulled the taco shells out of the oven and arranged them all on a plate.

"Where is that big bowl that mom has? I'll put the taco meat in that. And those little matching bowls will work to put the sour cream in. Is the hot sauce on the table already?"

"Nicolette, we're only having tacos. Calm down. Once the feeding frenzy starts, there will be too much chaos and mess for anyone to notice any of the serving dishes." Marie said.

"I doubt that makes her feel better, Marie. She's nervous enough as it is." Lisa added.

"When I brought Joe home to meet the family I was nervous too, but it worked out ok."

Nicolette turned and looked at her. "Was that before or after Dad farted at the table, Jerry started talking about Natalie's episiotomy, and Mom telling Pete and Frank to leave Joe alone after they jumped all over him for being a secretary?"

"He wasn't a secretary. He was an executive assistant for a year and half just until he could gain some experience and work his way up at the marketing firm." Marie said defensively.

"Yes, I know that and you know that, but that didn't stop them from asking him to bring them coffee and making innuendos about him taking dictation!"

Lisa burst out laughing. "Oh yeah, I forgot about that. That was funny."

Nicolette put the last bowl out onto the dining room table and walked back into the kitchen to quickly wash the pots and pans when the doorbell rang.

"I got it!" Frank yelled from the other room.

Nicolette turned her head from the sink and looked at Lisa. "Please go out and make sure he's nice?"

"I'm on it. Just quick wash the pans, so we can sit down and eat. The sooner we eat, the sooner you guys can get out of here. I'll worry about the after dinner dishes."

Nicolette left the pans on the drying rack next to the sink, dried her hands, and walked out into the living room. Ryan was sitting there talking to her Mom and Dad while Frank listened intently.

"Hi, Ryan. I'm sorry I wasn't out here to make introductions. Did you meet everyone?"

"Hi, I think so. I'm not sure I have all of the names memorized yet though."

Her mom responded before Nicolette could. "We always have a full house in the summer time, but we wouldn't have it any other way."

"Ryan can I get you something to drink?"

"Just water will be fine."

Frank chimed into the conversation. "We're all having Coronas since Nicky made Mexican food. Would you rather have one of those?"

"Sure, that sounds great."

"Dinner is ready everyone, so come on in to the dining room!"

Everyone sat around the table. Dad sat at the head of the table as always and Mom sat opposite him. Then Stephanie, Pete, Marie, Joe, Jerry and Natalie filed into one side of the table. Caitlyn, Nicolette, Ryan, Frank, and Lisa filed into the other. Everyone started passing bowls around and making their tacos. Frank was the first to ask a question. *Let the interrogation begin.*

"Ryan, what did you say your last name was?"

"Westin."

"What kind of work are you in?"

"I own my own construction company. My dad started it, but it was left to me when he passed away a couple of years ago."

"I'm sorry to hear that, Ryan." Mom said.

"Thank you, Mrs. Carson."

"Never mind all that 'Mrs. Carson' stuff. You can call me Linda."

"The name sounds familiar. Where is your company located?" Frank asked just before taking another bite of his taco.

"We're not far outside of Philadelphia. Our main headquarters is in Trevose."

"Your main headquarters?"

"We have ten crews that go out to different sites depending on where we're contracted. The office in Trevose is where we work out of."

"So that would be where you have your accounting and tax departments, right?"

Ryan straightened up in his seat. Then he calmly said, "Yes it is."

Caitlyn must have been bored with Frank's line of questioning, so she decided to jump in. "So if you own the company, you must be pretty rich huh?"

"Caitlyn! Where are your manners?" Mom asked.

"That's ok, Mom. Cate is probably just feeling a little out of whack. Cate, how's your stomach feeling? I know it was bothering you a little this morning."

"I'm fine, Nick. Thanks for asking." Caitlyn

shot Nicolette a look to kill.

"It's still no excuse for bad manners." Mom said.

"So Ryan, are you here on vacation?" Jerry moved to a safer topic. The other people at the table continued with their own conversations.

Natalie was describing childbirth to Marie since every night Marie thought of a new question to ask. "Oh yeah, I had an epidural. But let me tell you that once you start to tear, you feel everything so it doesn't make a damn bit of difference anyway. When I had Maya, I thought her head was the size of a cantaloupe when she was coming out."

"Oh my God, really? But your *you-know-what* eventually goes back to the way it was before though right?"

"Hopefully, but even if you're *that* lucky, nothing else will go back to the way it was. The summer after I had Nathan, every time I put on my bathing suit I looked up the name of a different plastic surgeon."

"But you look great and you never got any surgery."

"I have three words for you: personal trainer and under-wires. They will become your new best friends."

At that point, most of the table's attention turned back to Ryan. "I'm sorry Jerry, what was your question?"

"I'm not quite sure. Oh, I asked if you were here on vacation."

"Yes I am. A friend of mine owns a house over on 6th Street and he's letting me rent it for the week."

"That's nice. When are you here 'til?"

"I'll be here for a few more days."

At that point Nicolette's father took another sip of beer and let out a loud burp. All four kids started laughing from the other room.

"Ted, not at the table!" Nicolette's mother scolded her husband.

"Which one of you kids made that noise?" He yelled into the other room.

All of the kids laughed and said, "Grandpa! That was you!"

"I'm getting another Corona. Who wants one?" Joe asked.

Nicolette's father finished the rest of his beer, burped again, and said, "I'll take one, Joe."

"You absolutely will not. Joe, if you get him another beer you will sleep outside tonight." Her mother said.

Joe walked into the kitchen and Pete yelled in to him, "Get Dad a scotch and soda!"

"And hold the soda!" Her father added laughing.

"You all are going to be the death of me!" Nicolette's mother said setting down her glass with a bang.

Just when Nicolette thought that Ryan was out of the hot seat, at least for a few minutes, Frank chimed in. "Then will you go back to work or will you have other things to tend to?" He asked Ryan.

"I'll be right back to work. I have to keep the company running. As it is I've been working from my laptop at the beach house."

"Jerry has been working from here some days too." Stephanie told him.

Nicolette stuffed the last bite of taco in her mouth, stood up, and said that she was finished eating and asked if she could take anyone else's plate to the kitchen.

"Don't talk with your mouth full." Her mother corrected her.

"Yeah, it's rude." Her father said with a mouth full of taco.

"Ted!"

"Dad, ewww!"

"Oh my God, Dad that's so gross."

All the guys started laughing. Nicolette couldn't help laughing a little and to her relief, Ryan thought it was incredibly funny. She thought about when he told her that he didn't have any family. *He must be in shock over this mess.* When he stopped laughing, he started to get up from his chair. "I'll give you a hand with the dishes."

"No Ryan, please sit. You're a guest. I'll help Nicky with clearing the table." Frank told him.

"Nicky, didn't you say that you and Ryan wanted to go and get some ice cream after dinner?" Lisa asked already knowing the answer.

"Yeah, we were going to walk up to Dairy Delight and get some ice cream and then maybe take a walk down to the beach."

"Well then just leave the plates in the kitchen and Frank and I will take care of them." Lisa gave Frank a sharp look.

"Thanks, Lisa."

"As long as you help me clear the table first." Frank said.

Nicolette collected plates from the people who were done. Marie and Natalie weren't finished yet because they were still having their conversation about babies. They had moved onto the subject of what breastfeeding does to a woman's nipples. Pete and Joe were finished, but barely took notice of their plates being taken because they were having an in-depth conversation about why the Phillies shouldn't have made their latest trade. Dad ignored his wife and daughters' protests to him farting and joined in their conversation.

Nicolette took the stack of plates into the

kitchen with Frank behind her carrying items from the table.

"What the hell was that about?" Nicolette whispered to him.

"Oh my God, Nick. Pick up a paper one of these days. That guy was in court for the last two months being investigated for tax fraud. He's a crooked businessman."

"What?"

"Yes, you didn't know that?"

"No. Was he guilty of tax fraud?"

"It hasn't been settled yet."

"He never said anything about that to me. Look Frank, you know how much I love you, but the overprotective big brother act is getting old and so am I. I'm twenty nine."

"I'm not being overprotective. I'm telling you there is something not right about this guy."

"Are you sure you're even thinking of the right person? And let me ask you this: Tax fraud is a serious offense, so if he's accused of it, why isn't he in jail?"

"Because he made bail. I'm getting bad vibes from him. You should be careful. This is not something you need to be dealing with after everything you went through before."

"That's right. I did go through a hell of a lot before. And because of all that, I haven't even been able to have a healthy friendship with a guy until about three days ago. I'm finally moving on with my life."

"I know. I'm sorry. I'm happy for you, but there are other men out there to move on to."

"Look, I'll talk to him about all of this tonight, believe me. After telling him what I went through with Derrick, I can't believe he would keep this from me."

"Yeah, there's probably a reason *why* he didn't tell you. Wait, you told him about Derrick?"

"Yes, I did. Now you've made it obvious that you know all of this and that we're in here discussing it. So if I promise to talk to him, will you let me handle this?"

"I guess. I hope you know what you're doing."

"Yes, I do. Thank you."

They both walked back into the dining room and Nicolette asked Ryan if he was ready to go. He said he was and thanked her parents for having him and said how nice it was to meet everyone. Dad and Frank both stood up to shake his hand and then he and Nicolette walked through the living room and out the front door.

Chapter 16

"Your family seems nice."

"Surprisingly they were almost on their good behavior tonight. I'm sorry about my brother Frank probing you with questions. I would apologize for Caitlyn too, but you just have to ignore her like everyone else does."

"It's ok. I'm sure he filled you in on why he was questioning me so much while you both were in the kitchen after dinner."

"He told me that he read about you in the paper. You were arrested for tax fraud, but bail was posted for you. What he didn't tell me was that you have been cleared of the charges."

Ryan looked at the sidewalk as they walked down the street.

"You haven't been cleared, have you? Is there still a chance you might go to jail?"

"Yes, there is still a chance."

"And after everything I shared with you, you didn't think that this would be something I would want to know about?"

"Look, it's not what you think. And I didn't know how to tell you before."

Nicolette stared at him with a serious and angry look. "Well, tell me now."

Ryan knew it was time to come clean. He wasn't sure exactly how much to tell her, but he figured it didn't matter since she might turn around and walk away even after the beginning.

"I didn't do anything wrong. Shortly after my father died our business accountant George retired. George worked with my father since he started the business. We never had to question him about anything. When he retired we brought in this new guy Jack Harrison. He was great at first. Our profits were up, business was good, and everything was running smoothly. A few months ago I found out that Jack was embezzling money from the company. The company's revenue was five percent higher than it had been in the past three years. We were doing a lot of business so it made sense. What I didn't know was that Jack was about as sleazy as they come. He was creating fake books, forging false tax returns to the IRS, and pocketing the money. Our revenue was actually up twenty percent, which is a number I *would* have questioned. But I didn't see that part of it because he was keeping fifteen percent."

"How did you not know? Why wouldn't you check his records?"

"You don't think I've asked myself the same questions a thousand times? Do you know what it takes to run a business? I was making sure that all seventy-five guys I had working out on the sites were being taken care of, not to mention the thirty employees I have working in the office. There are health insurance premiums, workman's compensation claims, and a shitload of other things that come across my desk every day."

"Why didn't you tell me any of this? Why is this just now coming up?"

"I wanted to tell you tonight over dinner, but then you invited me over to your house and I wasn't about to announce it in front of your family."

"So after everything I shared with you about my ex-boyfriend going to prison and what that entire situation did to me, you didn't think this was something I would want to know?"

"This is completely different. I'm innocent. I didn't do anything wrong or hurt anyone. And I spent two nights in jail. I wasn't sentenced to five years."

"But you still might go back anyway, right? You still could be sentenced?"

"I don't want to lie to you. It's a possibility. But Nicolette, look at me. I would never ask you to pay for what happens to me. I wouldn't ask you to wait or to come visit me."

"No, you would only let me begin to really care about you just before you might go to prison."

"I shouldn't go to prison because I'm innocent, but these days that doesn't matter."

"What are you talking about? If you really are innocent, can't a lawyer prove it in court? Aren't there ways of proving that this guy Jack was the one who did everything?"

They reached Ryan's house and sat on the front steps. Ryan sat with his elbows on his knees and pinched the bridge of his nose between his thumb and index finger.

"There are, but it's just not that simple. Nothing in life is that simple."

"Yeah, you're right about that. Look, I'm sorry I compared your situation to Derrick's. That was wrong. He was guilty of what he did. It was his fault and he was suffering the consequences for it."

"I'm sorry you had to go through it. I would never do that to you. That's why I didn't try to kiss you or make any kind of move on you. I knew it wouldn't be fair, but when you kissed me... I couldn't help myself from kissing you back. And I can't stop feeling like I want to do it all the time. But I could never intentionally do anything to hurt you."

"You can't say that when you've only known someone for less than a week. That's an impossible statement."

"Look, I came down here for the week to relax and to think. I wanted for one week to put the whole mess out of my mind, even though I didn't think it would be possible. But then I found out that it was. You're the only thing I've thought about. I have been able to block out everything else because I was too distracted by you... by falling in love with you."

Ryan pulled his hand away from his face and placed both hands next to him on the step, but he stared at the ground in front of him.

"Ryan, look at me."

He looked up and Nicolette looked so intently at his eyes that it seemed that she was trying to look through them like tiny windows.

"You really mean that, don't you?"

"Yes, I do. Nicolette Carson, I love you."

"I love you too."

Ryan leaned in and kissed her. It was a long, slow kiss.

"Nicolette, wait. There's something else I have

to tell you."

"What is it?"

"I had a meeting with Harold Shaw the other day."

"Harold Shaw? He's Derrick's father. Why the hell were you meeting with him?"

"He was the one who posted my bail."

"Why would he do that? How do you even know him?"

"Until last night, I only knew him as the asshole district attorney who allowed charges to be pressed against me. Then when you told me about Derrick, I realized Harold Shaw was also Derrick's father."

"Why would he post bail for you?"

"He knows I'm innocent. But he's trying to blackmail me. At first I had no idea why."

"How is he trying to blackmail you?"

"He's still angry at you. He still blames you for what happened to Derrick. He said that if I came here and made you have some kind of "accident" that he would keep me out of jail and that he would pay me one hundred thousand dollars for my trouble. But if I didn't, he would personally make sure I went to jail and stayed there for a long time. He told me to give him an answer by tomorrow."

"So you came here because you were thinking

about physically hurting me? Or did he want you to kill me?"

"He didn't specify. And I didn't come here to do anything to you. I was just going to lay low, enjoy my last week of freedom, and tell him that I came here but that I couldn't find you. He just wanted to see you punished for what he *thinks* you did to Derrick."

"You thought about it though. You had to have at least thought about it. For that kind of deal, the thought would have crossed my mind."

Ryan decided to continue with being completely honest with her. The truth was that he had thought about it. He didn't know if he could actually do it, but he had come to the shore to find out. He wanted to find out if he put himself close enough to the situation whether or not the courage to do it would come to him.

"I did think about it. I didn't think I could do it, but I wondered if I owed it to myself to try. And even if I didn't owe it to myself, I had a lot of other things to consider."

"What do you mean?"

"If I go to jail, what happens to Westin Construction? If the company goes under or falls into disarray, there are a lot of people with families who would lose their jobs, their income, and their health insurance. I had to stop thinking about how my decision was going to affect only me. There were a lot of other people to think about."

"So you were trying to justify doing something terrible to me by using the excuse that it would be for the greater good?"

"No, I'm trying to be honest with you about everything that was going through my mind when I came here. All the things I wanted to forget, but couldn't because there was too much riding on it. I'm haunted by nightmares too. I don't want to go back to jail. I also don't want everything my father worked for and built to be demolished with a hundred employees being trapped under the rubble. Plus, I felt completely alone and had no one I could turn to or trust. But then I met you. And after talking to you for only a little while on the beach the first night we met, the only thing I've worried about since then was that I don't want you to be hurt when I go back to jail. After I met you, I knew there was no way I could even consider Shaw's offer anymore."

"How do I know that I can trust everything you're telling me?"

"I went to see him yesterday. I went to his house and told him I refused to do it, but he wouldn't listen. Then, I called him today. I told him that I couldn't find you and that I wasn't going to look for you anymore because I couldn't hurt another person. I told him to go ahead and send me to prison."

"So you're willing to turn down one hundred thousand dollars and go to prison, just to protect me?"

"No. I would be willing to do that just to protect an innocent stranger, just like you were to me five days ago."

"Even though you just said that the thought crossed your mind."

"Yes, but you said it would have crossed yours too." But after meeting you on that beach by chance, getting to know you, and falling in love with you... Now, I would be willing to give up my life to protect you."

"I don't want you to do that. If you're innocent, why can't your lawyer prove it in court?"

"Maybe he can, but it will be a tough case for any lawyer to win. There's a bigger problem than that though."

"What do you mean?"

"No matter what happens to me, if I don't do what Shaw wants, he might send someone else after you who will."

"Maybe we could fake something happening to me? Then he won't send you to jail and he'll think that he somehow made me suffer for what I did."

"That would be really hard to do. In order to make it believable, we would have to do something extreme. I won't risk you getting hurt trying to stage some fake incident."

They talked for an hour. Nicolette made one suggestion after another as to what they could do about the situation. They both agreed that without any proof, going to the police was out of the question because Shaw was untouchable and then Ryan would be dead long before he made it to court. The situation seemed hopeless.

They were still sitting on the front steps. For the moment they were out of ideas.

Ryan stood up and reached down to take Nicolette's hand. "It's getting late. I had better walk you home."

She slowly stood up, but on the step above him so that they stayed eye-to-eye. She leaned in to kiss him for just a moment and then she leaned in even closer and whispered in his ear, "I don't want to go home. How about you just walk me inside?"

Ryan leaned back. He looked at her and smiled. Then he leaned in and whispered to her, "Because as soon as you said that, I lost all feeling in my legs."

They both burst out laughing, but just for a moment. Then Nicolette smiled and said, "Just wait," as she turned and walked up the stairs and across the porch to the front door.

He couldn't believe it. She didn't hate him. After the last few days had been so wonderful, he dropped a bomb on her and she could see past everything. He had never met anyone like her. He really did love her.

In one quick, quiet motion, Ryan snuck up the steps behind her and lifted her into his arms. She felt tiny in his arms. "I don't think I can."

Chapter 17

Nicolette felt her feet come out from underneath her. Ryan scooped her up. He opened the front door, turned, and carried her inside, kicking the door shut behind him. He carried her through the living room, dining room, and turned into the hallway that led to the bedroom.

When she had been sitting on the porch with him, she knew he was being honest. He didn't know which direction he was going to go in anymore than she did. She realized though that when she had looked into his eyes that she didn't care. Whatever happened in the days, weeks, and months to come, she felt happy there in that moment. She wanted one perfect night before she had to think of what was going to come.

He laid her gently onto the bed. She kicked off her shoes while he took his off too and then he was on top of her in one smooth motion. She spread her legs and wrapped them around his waist. She brushed her hands over his hips and then slowly pulled his shirt up revealing his smooth, rippling stomach and hard strong chest.

He leaned back and kneeled in front of her so that he could pull his shirt off over his head. Then he reached down and pulled her shirt off and waited for her long smooth hair to unwind from the straps and release it. As he reached his arms around her back to unfasten her bra, he kissed his way down from behind her ear to her collar bone, and to her soft, smooth breasts. Her bra released and he tossed it aside, so that he was free to caress her with his hands and tongue. He traced the pale bikini shaped lines on her skin.

He kissed her breasts and she felt the cool tingle of his breath on her moist skin. He removed her denim shorts and she closed her eyes as she felt him kiss her stomach. She felt him nip lightly at her hip bone as he moved to the side and kissed the top of her thigh and down and around to the inside of it. He switched from the inside of her left thigh to the inside of her right. She ached for him to take her panties off, especially as he ran his tongue around the outline of them.

He stood up off of the bed and started to undo his belt. She sat up and then kneeled on the bed in front of him and undid it for him. He pulled down his jeans and boxers and allowed his erection to spring free from them. He stood on the floor next to the bed and she kneeled on the edge of it. She leaned in and kissed his neck and chest as she slid her hand down to gently stroke him all the way up and all the way down.

She stood up on the bed and he reached up to pull off her panties. She stepped out of them with one foot, but as she stepped out with the other he swept her legs from underneath her and she fell back onto the springy mattress covered in a soft, billowy quilt. He leaned over her and she put her arms around his neck and her legs around his waist. He reached under her and cupped her firm butt in his hands and lifted her off the bed. Turning in one, smooth motion he pressed her back against the wall as he held her up around him.

She felt every inch of her body pressing against his. She felt him lower her down, so that he could slide himself inside of her. It was like nothing she ever felt and she moaned and exhaled at the same time. He held her up against the wall and thrust into her again and again, more quickly each time.

She felt his hot breath on her neck as she breathed harder and moaned more and more. "Oh God yes, harder," she pleaded. She could tell he was happy to oblige. She felt so good pressed up against him and wrapped around him. She started to moan really loud and her thigh muscles squeeze his waist. Her hands gripped his back and every bit of her tightened around him.

Oh please don't let him stop. I can feel it. Oh yes, here it comes!

Nicolette yelled out when her body exploded from the inside. Ryan thrust into her a few more times to make sure she was able to enjoy every bit of it. Then she felt him move backward and he sat down on the bed. She removed her legs from his waist and kneeled over him. They did this without letting him slip out of her. She pushed him down so that he lied on the bed on his back. She rhythmically moved her hips up and down and in a circular motion.

He slid his hands up to cup her perfect bouncing breasts. Then he reached his hand down between her legs to rub her as she moved up and down on him. This made her move quicker and harder. Her eyes closed and her breathing quickened. He continued to rub and she screamed out once and then twice. Finally he couldn't take it anymore. He rolled her over onto the bed onto her back and he climbed on top of her.

He moved so quickly, she barely realized what had happened until she felt him climb on top of her and put himself inside. She could barely breathe, but she didn't want it to ever stop. His voice deepened as he moaned and he yelled out, "Oh yes!" in a deep raspy grunt just before she felt him release himself inside of her.

She felt herself let go of him as he pulled himself from her. He lied down next to her on the bed and they both laid there trying to catch their breath. He rolled onto his side, propping himself up on his elbow. Then he leaned over and kissed her very lightly. They stared at each other for a moment and then his eyes wandered over her body and he traced the outlines of her breasts and stomach with his finger tips.

"You are so beautiful."

"You make me feel beautiful." She smiled.

"I've wanted to tell you that every second of every minute since the first time I saw you."

"Deep down, I think I've wanted to tell you just how handsome I think you are, but something just wouldn't let me admit it at first."

They laid there for a while in silence. Nicolette slipped her panties and bra back on and lied back down.

"I don't want to go yet."

"No one said you had to. No one said you had to put any clothes back on either. I was enjoying the view." He smiled.

Nicolette heard a muffled ringing coming from the other room.

"Oh shit, that's my phone. I'll be right back."

She walked back into the bedroom with her phone in her hand. She had received a text message from Lisa: "Just wanted 2 give u a heads up. Frank & Jerry r sitting in kitchen talking. I think they r waiting up 4 u."

Nicolette read the text out loud. Ryan thought for a moment before he responded. "Do you have to go home?"

"I don't want to."

"I don't want you to either, but I don't want your family to hate me."

"They won't hate you."

"Your brother Frank already isn't my biggest fan and if he's telling Jerry everything he told you, I'm sure he won't be either."

"You let me worry about my brothers. I'm an adult. I can make my own decisions, they need to realize that. I'm texting Lisa back to let her know that I won't be home tonight.

Nicolette: Thanks 4 the heads up. Tell them to go to bed, I'll be home early in the AM."

Lisa: Sure, let them shoot the messenger lol. I'll tell them. Have fun and be careful.

Nicolette: Ur the best ;)

Nicolette pressed send and lied back on the bed. They laid there for a few more minutes and then he leaned over and started kissing her again.

Bang! Bang! Bang!

She and Ryan jumped from the loud pounding on the front door. Then Nicolette said, "Oh I am going to kill them! How the hell did my brothers know this was your house?"

"Sshhh… Nicolette, I don't think that's your brothers."

Chapter 18

"Westin, you open this door or I'm coming in anyway."

"Oh shit! I didn't lock the doors. Here, take your clothes and hide in the closet. Don't make a sound and don't come out no matter what."

"What the hell is going on? Should we call 911?"

"Oh God no. Don't call 911. Please, you have to trust me. Just hide. I won't let anything happen to you, I swear."

They heard the front door swing open and the

booming voice once more. Nicolette grabbed her
clothes and shoes and ducked into the closet. Once
she was hidden, Ryan jumped up and went to run
into the other room, but as he opened the bedroom
door he saw Harold Shaw and Jack Harrison
standing outside of it.

"Jack? What the…"

Jack punched Ryan in the face before he could
even finish his question. Ryan was caught by
surprise and stumbled backward. Jack went at him
and hit him again and again. Ryan fell to the ground,
but instantly got back up. Then Jack hit him one
more time. Ryan hit the floor again and had a much
harder time trying to get back up.

Nicolette stayed huddled up behind the folded
closet door and tried not to move. She still had her
phone with her, but if she tried calling 911 they
would hear the call. She didn't know what to do. She
turned the volume on the phone to "Silence all,"
and opened a text addressed to Lisa, Frank, and Jerry.
She had to make sure they called 911 and didn't just
try to come there themselves. She prayed at least one
of them was still awake and sent the following text:
"At Ryans. 428 6th Street. 2 men broke in. Im hidden
in a closet. They r going 2 kill him. Call 911. Help."
She had another idea, but she was going to have to
turn the volume back up on her cell phone. She
prayed that none of them would respond to her text
in the mean time.

"What are you doing here, Shaw? I told you I
wouldn't do it! How did you find me here?"

"Don't worry about how I found you. I can find anyone I want to. And I don't want to hear that you're not going to do it, you've made that abundantly clear. I'm here because you backed out on our deal."

"It wasn't a deal. It was blackmail!"

"That's a small matter of semantics. I told you that if you didn't make that little bitch pay for what she did to my son that I would put you away for a very long time. And we both know you don't deserve to be there. The evidence points to Jack here from every direction. He was stupid. He got greedy. And he fucked up. But at least he has balls."

"Fine, then send me to prison, but leave me alone!"

Shaw pretended not to listen and spoke with his usual indifferent tone. "You could have cut the brake lines in her car. You could have just beaten on her for a while." He started laughing cynically. "You could have tied her down and fucked her. I didn't care! And I didn't ask for much, did I, Jack?"

"No, Sir."

"I posted a lot of money to bail you out and you can't do one little thing. Before I put you back in jail, tell me where she is. Jack is going to do the job that you couldn't."

"I don't know where she is."

Jack took a step forward and kicked Ryan. Nicolette could here Ryan coughing. She felt helpless. She couldn't just let them keep beating him.

Ryan wasn't helping his own situation either. "Your son was a spoiled little bitch! He got exactly what he asked for and now you're going to lock me up because I won't hurt an innocent person to avenge him."

"She killed my son!"

"YOU killed your son! You kept letting him off the hook and he never learned until he finally got what he deserved. No, like I said before… what he ASKED for."

"You know what? I'm not going to argue with you. You want to go to prison, that's fine with me. I'll let this crooked asshole accountant of yours walk free, and you can sit in a jail cell. But don't think you're going there in one piece. Jack, go ahead. Westin, I'll see you soon."

Nicolette peered through the crack in the folding closet doors. Jack gripped up Ryan, stood him up, and punched him again. Ryan tried to fight back, but Jack was bigger and stronger. Ryan crumpled and lied on the bedroom floor. Jack kept hitting him until he couldn't even get up at all.

Nicolette couldn't watch it anymore. Just as she was about to burst out from behind the closet door, Shaw came back into the room and ordered Jack to stop and stand Ryan up. Jack did as he was told and stood Ryan up against the wall. He held him there while Shaw moved around to Ryan's other side and put his face very close to Ryan's.

"Where is she?"

Ryan was out of breath and in a lot of pain. "What?"

"Where is she?"

"I said I don't know."

"Oh, then I guess this is yours?" Shaw held Nicolette's purse out in front of him.

Nicolette peered out the crack of the folding closet door. *Shit I forgot I left that in the living room.*

"No, I went to a bar last night and hooked up with a girl and she left that here."

"Bull shit."

Shaw opened the purse and dumped everything out of it onto the bed. He grabbed the wallet and pulled out the driver's license.

Shaw held it up to Jack and said, "She's here somewhere. Find her. I'm taking this lying son of a bitch with me."

Nicolette stood up. She didn't even know if the cops were coming or if her brothers and Lisa saw her text. But even if they didn't and the police weren't coming, she couldn't watch Ryan be punished anymore for something that wasn't his fault. A situation he had nothing to do with. She took a deep breath, summoned up all the courage she could, and opened the closet door.

"I'm right here."

"You little bitch... you've been hiding in there this whole time."

"Yes I have. Did you really send people to come after me? Are you that much of a coward? You're here. I'm here. Why don't you just cut out the middle men and grow some fucking balls. Your son sure as hell didn't have any."

Shaw stormed across the room and punched her. She hit the floor hard. He was on her in a second and grabbed her by the throat. "I'll kill you, you little cunt!"

Pain seared in Nicolette's throat and face. She couldn't breathe. She could here Ryan yelling in the background. She started to feel dizzy and Shaw's grip only got tighter and tighter. She tried to kick him. She reached out to try to go for his face, but his arms were longer than hers and she couldn't reach. She clawed at him as she gasped for air.

Something caught Shaw's attention. Shaw let go of Nicolette's neck and she turned over coughing and gasping for air. Red and blue lights flashed through the bedroom window from outside.

"Police! Freeze!"

"Stay on your knees and put your hands behind your head!"

The first officer ran over and cuffed Shaw and the second officer cuffed Jack. A third cuffed Ryan. Nicolette wanted to stop the officer. She tried to tell him not to cuff Ryan, but nothing would come out except a raspy whistling sound.

As the officer pulled Shaw's arms behind his back and cuffed his wrists, Shaw said, "Please help her. These men were trying to kill her. Sweetheart, you'll be ok. Help is here."

The policeman who was taking Shaw into custody tilted his head to the side and pushed the button on the radio attached to his shoulder. "We're clear, send in the medics. We have a woman in here that is injured, possibly a broken windpipe."

A detective walked in and immediately ran over to the cop putting Shaw in handcuffs. "Sanderson, what are you doing? Take those cuffs off of him now! He's a District attorney!"

Neither of the policemen saw Shaw look down and give Nicolette a wicked smile.

"I'm sorry, Detective." Sanderson bent down to unlock the cuffs.

"Mr. Shaw, I'm sorry about that. Please come with me."

"Ok, but please help her." Shaw pleaded.

As the detective started to escort Shaw out, he looked down at her. "Ma'am, don't try to talk. The paramedics just arrived. They're coming now to help you. Sanderson, stay with her."

Nicolette turned over and tried to reach for the closet, but couldn't.

"Ma'am, stay where you are. Don't move." Sanderson ordering Nicolette not to move made the detective turn back around.

Nicolette used all of her strength to crawl towards the closet. She reached her arm out.

"Freeze!" Sanderson stood over her and drew his gun. The detective ran over and did the same.

"Ma'am, stay still or we will open fire!"

Nicolette pushed the closet door open. There was nothing in it except her cell phone lying on the floor. The men lowered their weapons.

At that point Shaw was on the other side of the room. He saw the phone and quickly started to walk back over. "She doesn't want to go to the hospital without her cell phone. You know women and their phones. Sweetheart, let me get that for you and I'll bring it to you after you see a doctor." He bent over to get the phone, but Nicolette used all of the strength she had left and grabbed it first.

She pushed the play button on the screen. Shaw's voice could be heard coming through the phone. "Don't worry about how I found you. I can find anyone I want to. And I don't want to hear that you're not going to do it, you've made that abundantly clear. I'm here because you backed out on our deal."

Then they could hear Ryan say, "It wasn't a

deal… It was blackmail!"

The entire conversation repeated itself through Nicolette's phone. As the recording played, Nicolette couldn't keep her eyes open anymore. Everything went dark.

Chapter 19

The tight, metal cuffs made Ryan's wrists burn. He took solace in the fact that the detective re-cuffed Shaw. Ryan's face felt like it was on fire as it continued to swell and his entire body began to ache. The officers walked both he and Jack out of the bedroom and moved them aside so the paramedics could get through to Nicolette. All three men, Ryan, Jack, and Shaw, were read their rights, escorted outside, and put into three different squad cars.

Ryan could see Nicolette's family standing outside waiting amidst the chaos in the glow of the flashing blue and red lights. Only Lisa, Jerry, and Marie looked in his direction, the rest didn't make eye contact. Her parents, Stephanie, Pete, Frank, Joe, and Caitlyn all just stared at the front door waiting for the paramedics to come through with Nicolette.

He watched the front door also right up until the squad car he was in pulled away. He was taken to the police station where he stayed for over four hours answering questions. The detective had taken Nicolette's cell phone and made a copy of the recording, which contained Shaw's voice giving a full confession. However, Shaw was also at the police station that night giving the police a different story. The detective walked into the room and sat at the table across from Ryan.

"Mr. Westin, you were recently accused of tax fraud by Mr. Shaw. He claims you lured him to the house you were staying in using his late son's girlfriend as a hostage. He said that you and Mr. Harrison then threatened him and forced him to give all of the false statements recorded on the phone you took from her."

"Do you see what condition I am in? I was attacked. Does it look like I was the threatening one?"

"No, it doesn't. And luckily for you, Shaw claimed all of this as a desperate attempt to keep himself out of jail and his reputation intact. However, he must have forgotten parts of the conversation. Once we played the recording for him during his interrogation, he realized all the holes that were in his story that we were already aware of. As far as the charges of tax fraud against you, we have no control over that. I've been told that your lawyer is on his way and will advise you how to proceed with that. We are not pressing any charges against you at this time. We are releasing you and as long as Miss Carson's story matches yours then we will not be seeing you again anytime soon."

"Thank you, Detective. How is she?"

"I haven't been updated on her condition since she arrived at the hospital. I'm sorry."

"Can I go? I would like to go see if she's ok."

"We need you to sign a few more forms first and then you are free to go. Right this way."

Ryan took a cab from the police station to the Atlantic County Hospital. He went into the emergency room and asked the woman at the desk where he could find Nicolette Carson. She asked him if he was family. Before he could answer, he heard a voice behind him.

"What are you doing here?"

Ryan turned around. "Frank, Lisa, thank goodness I found you. Is she all right?"

"She would be much better if she hadn't met you." Frank took Lisa's hand and turned and walked out the double sliding automated doors.

Ryan ran outside after him. "Frank, wait. Please, just tell me if she's ok and I will explain everything to you."

Lisa pulled Frank's arm back. "At least hear

what he has to say, Frank."

Before Ryan could say anything, Jerry came running out of the doors. "Ryan! You're here just in time. Frank, Lisa, she's waking up. Ryan, follow me. She's asking for you."

Chapter 20

Jerry, Ryan, Frank, and Lisa ran back into the hospital and Jerry led them all onto the first elevator that came. He explained to Ryan what had happened.

"Initially they put a tube down her throat to help her breathe, but she's been breathing on her own for the last two hours. We've been waiting for her to wake up."

"And she's awake now?"

"Yes and she is talking, but she's struggling a little with it."

They walked into the room where Nicolette was

lying in bed. Her mother and father were sitting beside her bed. Stephanie was lying on the empty bed next to Nicolette's with her feet on Marie's lap because she was sitting on the foot of the bed facing Nicolette. Caitlyn paced the floor behind them in front of the window.

Ryan walked into the room and went to Nicolette's bedside. He leaned down and kissed her on the forehead. She reached her arm out from under the blanket and held his hand, pulling it next to her so she could rest her arm back on the bed.

She opened her mouth, but she had to speak very slowly and quietly. "What… did… police… say?"

"They locked up Shaw. Thanks to your recording on your cell, they had enough evidence to arrest him and lock him up until the initial hearing."

Nicolette's whole body relaxed and she smiled.

"Ryan, can you tell us what happened?" Mrs. Carson asked.

Ryan proceeded to tell her family the whole story starting with Shaw trying to blackmail him, to him accidently finding Nicolette on the beach, and finally to Shaw and Jack breaking into the house. He felt Nicolette squeeze his hand when he said they were in the bedroom when Shaw started banging on the front door. Ryan blushed because he got so caught up in telling the story that he almost forgot her parents were in the room.

"Ha ha! You little slut!" Caitlyn blurted out.

"Caitlyn, hush!" Her mother snapped.

"Shut… up… Preggers…"

Everyone in the room stood very still while their eyes traveled back and forth between their mother and Caitlyn.

"You all can stop staring. I already knew. Caitlyn Dear, congratulations. We'll all celebrate the coming of my new grandbaby when your sister gets home from the hospital. Ryan, please continue with the story."

Ryan continued on with Jack beating him to a pulp, Nicolette revealing that she had been hiding in the closet to Shaw, and everything the detective told him at the police station.

"Well, I'm just glad you both are safe and those awful men have been put where they belong." Mrs. Carson said. "Now, I think it's time for us to be getting home. Nicolette needs her rest."

"I'd like to stay here, if that's ok with you, Mrs. Carson?"

"It's ok with me as long as you call me Linda like I told you to and as long as it's ok with Nicolette of course."

Nicolette smiled again to let him know she wanted him to stay. One by one, everyone got up, hugged and kissed Nicolette, and walked out of the room. Frank told them all that he would be home in a little bit. He wanted to stay a little longer and Lisa agreed and said she would stay just a bit more too.

Caitlyn walked over to Nicolette. She leaned over, gently hugged her, and kissed her cheek. "You're a bitch, Nick… but I love you." Then Caitlyn smiled and walked out of the room.

Once everyone else left, only Nicolette, Ryan, Frank, and Lisa were in the room. Lisa walked over and sat in the chair next to Nicolette's bed. Both girls stayed perfectly still while they both stared at Frank who was standing across the foot of the bed from Ryan.

"Stop staring at me, I was just getting to it." Frank said to them before turning to Ryan. "I'm sorry for how I acted at dinner and when you got here. I jumped to conclusions before I gave you any kind of a chance to explain and I was wrong to do that." Frank extended his hand to offer Ryan a handshake.

"It's ok and thanks. If I had a sister, I'm sure I would have done the same things. I never wanted to put Nicolette in danger. And I'm sorry I did, even though it was an accident."

They shook hands and Frank turned to Lisa and Nicolette. "We should probably get going too. Nick, we'll be here first thing in the morning and we'll help you get home the day after that." Frank walked over and leaned down to hug Nicolette. "I love you."

"I… love… you… big… brother."

"Sshhh. Rest your voice, Sweetie." Lisa said as she hugged Nicolette lightly. Then she hugged Ryan as well and followed Frank out of the room.

Ryan sat next to Nicolette's bed for the rest of the night and the following morning. Nicolette continued to hold his hand and she fell back to sleep. Ryan took a pillow from the other bed to rest his head on and finally fell asleep too.

Chapter 21

At the end of June the following year, Ryan picked Nicolette up after school in his truck. They were going to meet her family at her parents' house at the shore. Nicolette stared out of the passenger side window as they pulled on to the Expressway. She couldn't wait to smell the salty air.

Ryan looked from the road to Nicolette and back again. "Why are you smiling?"

"I still can't believe what you did for Jerry after he was laid off from his job."

"Well, his company only laid him off because

he was making too much money. He's a brilliant businessman, so they got rid of him in order to hire a stupid businessman whom they could pay a much smaller salary to. Besides, he'll make a better CEO of Westin Construction than I ever could and I was much happier as a foreman going out on site than I ever was wearing a suit and tie into that office every day. Plus, I'm still a majority shareholder."

"You just continue to surprise me. I love you so much."

"I love you too, which is why I have another surprise for you."

"What is it?"

"You're going to have to wait to find out."

"That's not fair!" Nicolette laughed. "Tell me now."

"Well since we're almost ready to turn off the Expressway and we have to make a stop on the island before we get to your parents' house, I guess I have time to tell you. You know how last month I had to go back to court?"

"Yes, but you said that was just another hearing and that it was nothing to worry about."

"It wasn't something to worry about. It was a settlement hearing. I had to go to court to find out that the DA's office is granting me a very large settlement in my suit against them."

"Oh Ryan, that's so wonderful!

Congratulations! Wait, why are you turning this way? My parents' house is a couple blocks up. Where are we stopping?"

"Don't worry. I'll stop before I hit the ocean."

"Are you sure? There's the dead end and 2nd Street entrance to the ocean."

"I know. We're almost there."

Ryan pulled the truck over and parked next to the curb. He walked around the truck to open Nicolette's door and help her out.

"What are we doing?"

Ryan pointed across the street. "Do you see that house right there, the first one off of the beach?"

"Yeah."

"Do you see the one next to it?"

"The big one that someone painted bright orange?"

"That is a hideous color isn't. Maybe you could pick out a new color for it?"

Nicolette looked more closely at the house and noticed the real estate sign on the lawn with the rectangular tag across it that read "sold" on it. She spun around and looked at Ryan in shock. He stood there holding up a set of keys with a big smile spread across his face.

"You bought a beach house?!? Are you

kidding? This is amazing!"

"Do you want to go see the inside?"

"Of course!" Nicolette grabbed his hand and ran across the street.

Ryan unlocked the door and Nicolette walked through the empty rooms looking at them in awe.

Ryan followed her and said, "It will look much nicer once it's furnished."

"It's perfect."

"Come on, I'll show you the upstairs."

Ryan led Nicolette upstairs and she walked down the hallway. Ryan pointed out the bathroom, and the two guest rooms, all of which were empty. Then Ryan told Nicolette she had to see the view of the ocean from the master bedroom. He walked in front of her and opened the double doors for her.

Nicolette didn't know what to say. She looked around the magnificent room. It had in it a king sized sleigh bed and gorgeous matching furniture. Light poured in the large bay windows on the far and right walls revealing the beautiful and subtle color schemes of light blue, light green and different shades of mocha and beige.

She walked over to the bed, which was covered with white rose petals and picked up the little velvet box sitting in the middle of them. She opened the box and turned back around to look at Ryan who was kneeling behind her on one knee.

"I thought this house would make a nice engagement present. I bought it for you."

"I don't know what to say."

"I'm hoping that you'll say yes in a few seconds. Nicolette Carson, Will you marry me?"

"Yes."

ABOUT THE AUTHOR

Carrie Watson is from Oaklyn, NJ. She attended Camden Catholic High School in Cherry Hill, New Jersey. She earned her Associate's Degree from Camden County College and then went on to earn her Bachelor's Degree in Writing Arts from Rowan University. She started writing poetry in 2003, but soon after found her passion in writing short fiction. *At Low Tide* is her first novella of literary fiction to be published.